two and a half rivers

ANIRUDH KALA

NIYOGI
BOOKS

Published by
NIYOGI BOOKS
Block D, Building No. 77,
Okhla Industrial Area, Phase-I,
New Delhi-110 020, INDIA
Tel: 91-11-26816301, 26818960
Email: niyogibooks@gmail.com
Website: www.niyogibooksindia.com

Text © Anirudh Kala

Editor: Arunima Ghosh
Design: Shashi Bhushan Prasad
Cover design: Misha Oberoi

ISBN: 978-93-91125-20-2
Publication: 2021

Printed at Niyogi Offset Pvt. Ltd., New Delhi, India

This book is dedicated to the memory of those four hundred and eighty farmers and farm workers, who have so far died while protesting, on the borders of Delhi, against the new farm laws.

Advance Praise

'How do you tell of the tragedy of a state, ravaged by political tensions and a religious war? Anirudh Kala offers us three unforgettable characters, a depressive doctor, and a young Dalit couple who are struggling with an oppression that is centuries old and completely indifferent to the promises of Guru Nanak. Punjab has found its Graham Greene and its Bohumil Hrabal.'

Jerry Pinto,
Author of *Em and the Big Hoom*

•

'Keenly observed, wryly written, *Two and a Half Rivers lays bare the schisms of Punjab in this masterly tale by Anirudh Kala.*'

Manreet Sodhi Someshwar,
Author of *Radiance of A Thousand Suns*

•

'A feisty exploration of the militancy years of Punjab. With rare sensitivity, courage and sagacity Kala explores the many dimensions of the complex violence of those dark decades.'

Amandeep Sandhu,
Author of *Panjab: Journeys Through Fault Lines*

One

She was sixteen when I saw her for the first time, lying unconscious on the examination table in my small clinic, one summer night. Once again, what had woken up her dorm mates in the girls' hostel was the sound of her trying to force open the door, which was merely bolted from inside. They could hear the sound even in their sleep, despite the loud desert cooler, because she was persistent. Her eyes were open and face, blank of any expression. The girls were used to her sleepwalking every few nights and they escorted her gently back to her bed, where, as always, she murmured something about a dancing hall, before lying down obediently. But what followed that night frightened them, because they had never seen that before. Her face turned to one side like that of a broken rag doll and her body had gone into a spasm. Fists could not be opened even with force, and her arms and legs thrashed, shaking the bed, after which her body became limp, and her breathing, loud and laboured. Lights came on in the whole block and panic spread when the girl could not be woken up. The warden and three other students had brought her to me in a ramshackle car. Not because I was the best doctor around, but because I was the only doctor for miles. Everyone knew that I lived above my clinic, which was on the same side of the river as the school, just 5 km downstream. Their regular doctor, who came for two hours every afternoon, lived in the city on the other side of the river. And the nearest bridge across the river was 8 km away.

She lay there still, a dark frail girl, with her long hair open, in a blue salwar, probably part of her school uniform and a white 'chemise'. Blood had dried at one corner of her mouth from her having bitten her tongue during the seizure.

It was obvious that she had an epileptic fit. I did what needed to be done, which was giving an injection to prevent another attack, cleaning the congealed blood inside her mouth and turning her on her side. Her breathing became easy. By the time she woke up, it was morning and, apart from the perplexity about her surroundings and slurred speech as a result of the sedation and the tongue bite, she was fine. I explained to the warden about her condition as best as I could. That it was the normal electric impulses in the brain going haywire for a few seconds. Like a short circuit, I said. The warden was well-informed herself, having seen many young students—teenagers—have seizures, that being the age at which epilepsy often started. I wrote out a prescription and suggested some tests since the girl looked anaemic, although that had nothing to do with epilepsy.

She came again, on a cycle, three days later, to show me the test reports, with a maid from the hostel sitting behind her on the carrier. It was mid-morning, but the road already glistened in the heat and it was difficult to look at the expanse of sand on the riverbank because of the glare. I gave them some water and scolded her for having cycled 5 km with a pillion rider in the blazing heat, a mere couple of days after a seizure. I added some iron tablets to the prescription and gave her the standard advice given to kids with epilepsy. 'Do not miss the medicines. If you forget a dose, take it whenever you remember. Do not stay up late, do not swim till you have not had a fit for at least six months and, then too, under supervision. Do not watch TV for more than an hour a day and avoid all flickering lights.' I tried to make it sound light-hearted. But I was also firm. I had been told, I was good with children.

Her brow clouded several times during the conversation, but would clear after a moment. In a manner more thorough than most adults, she asked me questions about her condition and the limitations it might cause to her routine. I assured her that once her body got adjusted to the medicines, those would be very few. Usually, parents asked me these questions. I wanted to know if the warden had informed her family and how they had taken it. She told me, without a hint of self-pity, that she had no family; her mother had died when she was young and her father died last year of lung cancer. 'From smoking too many beedis,' she added with the nonchalance adolescents often put on as a front. She was a pretty girl: thin, dark, and tall, with sharp features and large expressive eyes, the sort which looked kajal-lined even when they are not. Over the next couple of weeks, I noticed that she would talk in a spirited manner when telling me stories about her friends in the hostel and the games they played. But when it came to her father's cancer and his death in the government hospital, her face would be impassive and her speech, deadpan, as though she was reading the weather. The obligatory body movements were all there, but the voice was empty of any emotion. Bheem, a boy from her village, who was with her in the primary and middle school, was her only connection to the village now. He came to her school to meet her and to give her the rent money from the one-room dwelling in the village, which she inherited after her father died. With this sum, she paid for her tuition and the hostel fees—an amount not too high, as it was a government school. Why she did not join the high school near her village and save the hostel money, I asked. Her answer, 'This is the nearest government school which has a dance teacher', was as unusual as the 16-year-old herself: alone, independent, house owner of sorts, with a steady boyfriend. The last bit of information she gave me on her fourth or fifth visit, when she had come alone on her cycle.

I was out buying vegetables, and upon my return, found her upstairs in my kitchen looking for drinking water.

'Medicines make me thirsty. The hand pump downstairs is not working,' she explained.

Two

It was an abrupt and a heavy shower. More like a cloud burst. The 50-year-old worn out roof of the government middle school started leaking like a sieve when sheets of water hit it. The kuccha floor of one of the two classrooms was soon awash with puddles. The other classroom was under this one, on the ground floor, where six- and seven-year-olds repeated multiplication tables after the teacher, in a sing-song fashion. Since the school had just one teacher, the younger children were being monitored by the class captain, a child selected more for heft than intelligence.

Shamsie moved her frayed mat nearer to the wall, as did the other children, and craned her head above Bheem's, which blocked her view now, of the three different maps of the state drawn on the blackboard. The racket of the rain on the roof, the singing of nines into sevens downstairs, the honking and screeching of buses on the road, and the shouting by hawkers just below the window formed a confounding medley of sounds. It was a poorly funded village school, located right on a busy highway. Over the years, the road had widened and the school had shrunk. The playground was long gone, and now, the buses stopped outside the classrooms; the conductors hailing passengers competed with the chanting of multiplication tables. The teacher, Batta, was a gruff and cynical man. The government has no money to fund the school or anything else for that matter, he explained. God knows what they do with the money. Of course, the students did not understand.

Right now, Harbans Lal Batta was struggling to be heard. He was telling them about how Punjab had shrunk in size over the decades. Shamsie did not catch most of it because of the ruckus, and thanks to Bheem's stupid head, she could barely see the maps. Suddenly, the drip of water from the ceiling became a flow and the teacher was forced to call off the school for the day.

There goes the dal and bread, thought Shamsie. A watery dal and a slice of bread was the grandly termed 'mid-day meal' in government records. Shamsie had only tea for breakfast and was hungry. She glanced enviously at the *pinni* (a Punjabi sweet made of flour and almonds) that Harpreet, the fairest girl in their class, had taken out of her brass tiffin, which she was now sharing with her younger brother. Shamsie rolled the mat, collected her slate and chalks, and pushed these into her bag. Nobody could leave right then, because of the torrent, and Bheem could not go home for another hour in any case. He would spend this time cleaning the teacher's living quarters next to the school and doing laundry for his family, which included the laundry of the teacher's son who was sitting two rows away on a *pukka* patch of the floor. Teachers sometimes made Dalit students do all their household chores. Without payment of course. This was an old tradition. Shamsie, being a girl, was exempted. This had nothing to do with any sensitivity to her gender. It was a precaution, to avoid a scandal like the one that had occurred during the tenure of the previous teacher.

Bheem and Shamsie were the only Dalit students in the school. The others were from a different world, children of landowning Jats, except two boys and a girl from a large family of Banias that owned the grocery shop in the village and a ration depot in the bazaar. All the other Dalit children of the village worked with their parents. The men worked as farm labourers called 'seerins' in fields they did not own, mostly for a pittance. The women cleaned the homes of the Jats and the Banias. The boys grazed cattle belonging to Jats and the girls ran after the cattle the whole day to gather dung. They collected the dung in iron basins, which they carried on their heads. Later, they would shape it into large cakes and slap them on the outsides of their walls to dry, to be used as fuel in their homes.

Not just Jats, even Dalits made no bones about the utter foolhardiness of Bheem and Shamsie's parents in trying to rise above their caste by sending their children to school. What did they expect them to become? Deputy Commissioners? They asked.

The sprawling 'Vehra', which actually means a court yard, was a ghetto within the village where the Dalits lived.

From the Vehra, just these two children, among perhaps a hundred, walked out with school bags every morning.

Bheem was born six years after Comrade Ramchander's marriage, a much-anticipated product of his wife's third pregnancy, the earlier two having been still births. Ramchander worked as a leather tanner in Jalandhar, an hour away by bus. The city was the seat of a sprawling army cantonment. Since the army required shoes and belts in large numbers, a mammoth leather industry had spawned, which involved a range of business activities from skinning dead cattle to packaging shoes and belts. Ramchander worked late and was mostly away from home. Bheem's mother, a cleaner at a Jat house, returned from work only in the evening after her employers had eaten and she had washed the utensils. She was not allowed to cook for them. That was done by a widowed relative.

'Vehra' was a generic word and most villages had one. Its only function was to contain the low-caste dwellings effectively, so that there was no spill over into the rest of the village, which, in this case, was occupied by Jat Sikhs, a few Banias, and the eccentric, semi-literate Brahmin who did nothing more than draw squares and crosses on paper and give out prophesies to gullible women. He also sold them fake gems of red, blue, and pistachio colours to make their problems, like childlessness, abusiveness of mothers-in-law, and waywardness of husbands, go away. He also conducted weddings at the Bania households. The city Brahmins were more prosperous and slightly better at scriptures, because in the cities, Hindus outnumbered Sikhs. There was more work for them there and the households were more discerning.

The Vehra itself was a squalid, overcrowded place. Mud and brick shanties, with cow dung cakes on the walls, surrounded a middle space traversed during the day by unclean children, hens, stray dogs, a drunk or two, and some adolescents trying to have a party out of a clump of cannabis leaves they had collected while grazing cattle. A strong smell of cow dung hung in the air day and night.

This Vehra stood to the west of the main village, so that the rays of the rising sun reached Jat homes directly, without being polluted by the Dalits. The dirty water drain ran from east to west, based on the same fuzzy logic. In the years that this part of the story is based, that tradition was still enforced rigidly.

The shower quickly became a drizzle. Nine-year-old Shamsie, satchel strapped to her back, walked in rubber flip flops to her father's workplace to collect the key to their house. She was a lanky, vivacious child, tall for her age, and dark-skinned like all Dalits. As the saying was, you could not have a dark Brahmin or a fair Dalit. Perched on a squat mound of earth half a mile away, the village could be seen even from her school. This was the reason it was called Uccha Pind, a village higher than the flat landscape surrounding it for miles.

Shamsie's father was a sweeper at the new museum which had opened the previous summer. A sweeper not of the halls, where the freshly-mounted statues, figurines, slabs, and coins stood on display, but the sweeper of the toilets, outside the main block. The toilets catered to a staff of 10 and a trickle of visitors. Most visitors were motorists on long journeys, whose cars turned in from the highway for them to pee, stretch their limbs, drink a cup of tea, and have a quick dekko at the long-lost heritage, all in 20 minutes or so. Photography was prohibited inside the museum, but was allowed at the Buddhist stupa nearby, which had come up as a chance discovery, surprising even the archaeologists. Another came up later near the village. Most of the artefacts were from the prehistoric Harappan civilization, said to be three or four thousand years old. But the stupas were remains of Buddhist prayer centres of the more recent Kushana Empire. Occasionally, some foreigners came, who stayed in the city, but spent the day at the museum. Most were archaeology students and researchers, who had to get special permission from Chandigarh to take a certain number of pictures inside the museum.

***

Three years ago, one early morning, the villagers had been taken aback to be the centre of a sudden attraction. Tents were being pegged over a large area outside the village. About a dozen men in hats and safari suits, brought in a long bus, were supervising the arrangements. The sarpanch was informed that the team of archaeologists that had come the previous summer was fairly convinced that the mound on which the village stood as well as the fields around it had deep under them, the remains of a whole civilization from thousands of years ago. And the new team had now come to follow up on that. The 'dig' or 'khudai', as it came to be called, lasted two years. Fields around the village were temporarily taken over by the government through a special order and dug up in the following weeks. The farmers were compensated for the loss of crops. In addition to the permanent team, archaeologists from around the world took to dropping in frequently, once artefacts started to turn up. The white visitors in straw hats and dark glasses, going about the village followed by a gaggle of curious children, became a common sight.

The law did not permit the government to acquire houses, but lanes could be dug up and that made life difficult for the villagers. It was noisy and meddlesome. And it blocked the lanes. The smell of diesel needed to run the drilling machines and generators made things unbearable. But the villagers, happy with the attention, tried to cooperate...till the workers, perched high up on rigs, looked down into the courtyards and the women screamed bloody murder at being ogled in their own homes. The villagers blocked the *khudai* and threw everyone out. It was resumed only after a hurriedly constituted committee of village elders and members of the archaeology team met and gave a solemn promise that they would be mindful of women's privacy and that there will be a minimal disruption in the villagers' daily routines.

Fragmented remains of a palace started being hauled up the shafts that had been sunk deep into the ground in all the village streets. The comprehensive statement released when the *khudai* ended, parts of which even made it to the international news, reported that priceless remains of the Harappan Civilization and of the Kushan Empire had been found in unexpectedly large numbers from a vast area extending up to a thousand yards from the village.

Since it was impossible to transport stupas to the city, experts advised the government to construct an onsite museum near them, where all the other excavated artefacts could be displayed. This, in hindsight, was considered unwise, since the only visitors the far-away museum received were the intercity commuters in a hurry and the occasional researcher. Archaeologists, like all academicians, it seemed, were bad marketeers.

***

By the time Shamsie reached the tall museum gate with its 'Archaeological Survey of India' sign, the back of her salwar was covered with splash from her slippers. The parking lot was chockful with mud-spattered cars. She passed the tea stall where the famished commuters jostled for samosas. At the ticket window, five people stood quietly in a queue as if in awe of history.

Children born in the lowest castes are more likely to be named after gods, goddesses, and celebrities by their parents. Or simply as Raja or Rani. Bheem was named after the Dalit jurist Bhim Rao Ambedkar, known world over as the 'father' of the Indian Constitution. Ironically, after having drafted the constitution, Ambedkar walked out of the fold of Hinduism as a protest against its caste prejudice by converting to Buddhism.

Krishan, Shamsie's father, was named after Lord Krishna, while her grandfather, a leather tanner, was named Shiva. Shiva's father was Raj Kumar, the Hindi word for prince, and Bheem's father shared his name with Lord Rama himself. These hallowed names were among the few things Dalit parents could give their children without any hindrance or expense. So, they went all the way.

Shamsie walked to the patch of green between the ladies and gents toilets, where Krishan was sitting on his haunches, smoking a beedi, his broom and wet mop perched against a wall. He flicked away the burning end and put the rest of the beedi into a fold of his blue *parna* wrapped around his head. He stood up to kiss her gently on her head, taking care not to let his hands touch her although there was nothing wrong with them. It was just the way visitors gave him way made him feel unclean.

Krishan was a second-generation refugee from Pakistan. His grandfather, Raj Kumar, the prince, had given up his work of skinning cattle carcasses and joined the army, when the Second World War started. This, he thought, would be a masterstroke towards shedding his Dalit ancestry. And for three years, as he fought for the Crown, first in Africa, and then in Burma, Raj Kumar believed he had succeeded. Until, in a cruel twist of fate, the British army constituted a brand new separate Chamar Regiment for the people of his caste. The Irish brigadier, who floated the idea, argued that ethnicity-based battalions fought better because of the sense of belonging so created, and the cohesiveness it imparted to the battalion. Inspired by this logic, a Chamar Regiment was formed to replicate the successes of the exclusive Sikh, Jat, Dogra, and Gorkha regiments. And yet, the Irish Brigadier was wrong. For while the Dogras, Sikhs, Jats, and Gorkhas had wanted to belong, the Chamars had joined the army for the exact opposite reason, to 'disbelong' and forget that they were Chamars. They wanted to be assimilated in the vast behemoth that was the British Indian Army, never to be recognized by their caste again.

Naib Subedar Raj Kumar then found himself posted in the Chamar Regiment as one of its unwilling founding members. He was a soldier of the British Army, but once again, a Chamar. Raj Kumar, the prince, died on the Kohima front three years later. His death was not due to a Japanese bullet, but because of leaping off a cliff into the Tizu River. Raj Kumar took this drastic step after weeks of complaining to the unit doctor of being chased by dead cattle all over the hills. And of hearing taunting voices of his ancestors mocking him, 'If it were so easy, do you think we were idiots for never having done something about it?' In a further twist of irony, the war ended three months later. The Chamar Regiment was disbanded, and the soldiers, absorbed back into their parent units. The official reason given in army files for disbanding the Chamar Regiment, even as the Sikh, Jat, Gorkha, and Dogra regiments carried on as before, was 'unforeseen circumstances'.

Raj Kumar's son and Krishan's father, Shiva, was 15 at the time, and worked with a hide tanner in a village near Sargodha. Shiva had a difficult choice of his own to make a few years later, when the Partition of India happened. The dilemma was whether to change the religion, become a Muslim, and continue living in the newly carved out Pakistan, or, to keep the Hindu faith and go to India. Most from his caste chose to stay. They reasoned that a Hindu leather worker is the same as a Muslim leather worker. It made little sense for them to move to a strange country and risk being slaughtered on the way. And that risk they had heard was substantial.

Shiva, however, carried himself and his religion safely across a flaming border. His caste too came along, written in Urdu on the inside cover page of his ration card. But Shiva was happy to be alive. He spent the rest of his life skinning carcasses, very much like he did in the Sargodha village that he had left behind.

His only child, Krishan, fought his own battle like his grandfather to break free of the caste mould. At the factory, where he went to sell cow hides, someone told him that there were no castes in Sikhism. They said that this is what was written in Guru Granth Sahib, the holy book of the Sikhs, '*Awwal allah noor upaya qudrat keh sub banday, aik noor keh sab jag upajiya kaun bhale ko mande.'* The Sikh accountant in the factory translated it for him. 'All humanity was born from a single divine light and everybody is born equal. All are the children of Nature and no one is good nor bad.'

These words touched Krishan's simple heart. That same day, he started growing his hair and stopped shaving. He quit smoking beedis and put on a decent turban. Once the beard was presentable, he took a bus from the school bus stop on the highway and went to the Golden Temple in Amritsar. He returned a baptized Sikh, wearing the kara, a sturdy steel bangle, and the kirpan, a small scimitar around his waist. He had learnt a bit of the scriptures and named his two-year-old daughter Gurshamsheer, which meant 'the Guru's sword'. His own name, after three months' time and at a cost of 50 rupees for the declaration in the Punjabi newspaper, got changed from Krishan Kumar to Krishan Singh.

Eight years later, however, Krishan Singh was still not allowed to join langar, the community meal after prayers, at the big gurdwara. He could often be seen arguing with the blue robed guards, 'Guru said, *qudrat de sab bande.* Everybody is allowed. Even Muslims.' Each time, he was curtly told, 'Muslims are. Chamars are not.'

'But I am a properly baptized Amritdhari Sikh,' he would insist, pointing one by one to his turban, his beard, and the kirpan, as if explaining to a child. 'You are a Sikh, but a Chamar Sikh. This is a Jat gurudwara. You have your own Gurudwara in the Vehra; go there'—would be the response.

At the newly opened museum, where Krishan was hired as a sweeper, he was confined to the outdoor toilets. His entry into the hallowed sanctum sanctorum, where statues of stylish women from thousands of years back reigned, was forbidden. A higher-caste cleaner was hired for the indoors. Krishan insisted that he be shown the rule that said that he was not allowed inside the halls. He was told that there was nothing written, only verbal orders from the staunchly Brahmin director of the department whose office was in the capital. A miffed Krishan took off his kirpan, cut his hair, shaved off his beard, and bought ten packets of beedis at one go. It would have been too cumbersome to rename his schoolgoing daughter. She continued to be Gurshamsheer Kaur in the school register, but was called Shamsie by everybody. His own name too continued being Krishan Singh. Technically, it was possible to change it back, but the process was too tedious and now costed 100 rupees. He was too worn out to bother.

Krishan went with Shamsie into the men's toilet and prised out the house key from behind the pipe under the wash basin.

On the way to the village, the mud track was all slush. Shamsie tiptoed on the narrow parapet of the mustard fields, which were awash in yellow as far as the eye could see. With the school bag on her back, she walked with her arms stretched out for balance. From a distance, she looked like a marionette to Bheem, who had completed his work at the teacher's house rather quickly.

Krishan would not be home till the evening and all Shamsie could make was a cup of tea. 'Let us go to the big gurudwara. Today is *sangrand*; there will be food,' she told Bheem.

The 'big gurudwara' was the Jat gurudwara at the far end of the village and stood majestic in the distance from where they were. In celebration of *sangrand*, the first day of a month in the Indian calendar, loudspeakers pointing in all four directions filled the air with musical hymns. The small Vehra gurudwara would have celebrations and lots of people too. But, from experience, the two children knew there would be no food there.

Once they reached the big gurudwara, the Nihang guard shouted at them, 'This gurudwara is not for people like you. Why don't you go to your own?' Bheem looked up brazenly at the tall man in flowing robes. The Nihang looked even taller with his large turban and its elaborate steel emblem of a curved moon and a double-edged sword.

'Baba Nanak said that all are born equal. *Aik noor ton sab jag upjiya, qudrat de sab bande,*' Bheem recited like the younger children chanted multiplication tables in school. All the Vehra kids had memorized this stanza of Baba Nanak's 'Qudrat de sab bande' for such occasions. Except these words carried no weight in the real world. Like the ancient clay coins the children picked up lying around during the *khudai*, and which experts valued but which the shopkeepers threw back at them saying, '*Eh apni maan nu deyin* (give it to your mother).'

The Nihang apparently relented, 'Fine then, big lawyer, go through the back entrance, the one meant for your sort.' But both Shamsie and Bheem knew they were being fobbed off and that the back door was locked on a *sangrand* day. The two ducked and ran past him. They had done it before and were soon hidden behind the baggy trousers of a gaggle of worshippers from Canada. Unknown to them, the kids had left a commotion behind them. The Nihang, who could not leave his post, asked a passing *sewadar* to find the children. When the *sewadar* asked for their description, he was rebuked, 'Are you blind? How difficult is it to spot Vehra kids?'

Both Shamsie and Bheem were much darker than the other children in their class. Bheem came from a stock even lower than Shamsie on the caste ladder, that of the scavengers. But he happened to be a shade fairer than her, which she teased him about—'No justice, even though I come from a caste higher than yours...'

Krishan, who came from the tanners' caste, worked as a sweeper, and Bheem's father, whose ancestors were sweepers, worked as a tanner in a factory. At the time, the two children found it perplexing. As they grew up, they found that for upper caste people, all those on rungs lower than them were Chamars. It was convenient that way.

Their teacher, Master Batta, was a cleanliness freak. Once in every week, he would line up students to inspect their nails. Shamsie and Bheem would have their fingers twisted and wrists slapped more often than the others. Since one was motherless and the other's mother left for work at 6 in the morning, their nails were often unclipped and the hair a mess. For Master Batta, these two kids were like fish in a tub that he could pick out anytime. On the rare occasion the two had their hair oiled, he would scold other unkempt children saying, 'You should be ashamed of yourself. Even Bheem and Shamsie are not as dirty as you are.'

Bheem and Shamsie sat quietly on the floor of the big gurudwara, their heads covered and hands folded, in the middle of the congregation, trying to be invisible. They waited patiently for the kirtan to end, after which langar would be served in the hall at the back. But as ill luck would have it, at the end of the *ardas*, they discovered that it was the young *sewadar* deputed to find them whose turn it was to distribute the prasad. When he came to them, the two cupped their palms together to receive the sweet halwa. But either due to the small size of Bheem's hands or the irate man was being too careful to avoid touching the skin of an untouchable, the halwa fell off from Bheem's cupped palms to the dust-filled durrie. Bheem was pulled out and taken outside the gate, where the Nihang slapped him hard, 'This is for insulting the guru's prasad. Don't show your dark faces here ever again.'

Both Bheem and Shamsie knew that it was a charade to deny them langar. Bheem's face was blanched with anger. Even as he walked away, he glared back at the tall figure in blue robes, who soon went back through the enormous entrance of the gurudwara.

Three

Back on the road to the bazaar, Shamsie gave Bheem half of her bit of halwa. His anger at the Nihang having dissipated, Bheem sang while walking zigzag on the parapet, '*O, kala doria kunde naal arhya ee oye, ke chhota devra bhabi naal ladya ee oye* (the black cord got stuck in the door and the younger brother of my lover fought with me).'

'Want to have jalebis?' Bheem asked. Since lunch at the gurudwara was no longer an option and Krishan would not be back for three hours, Shamsie nodded.

At the sweetshop in the bustling street, they asked for jalebis. The man took one look at the two dark children in faded, mud-spattered school uniforms and wanted to see money first. After Bheem had paid with a crisp five rupees note, Shamsie asked, 'Where did you get it?'

'I earned it,' he said looking straight back at her.

'How?' she wanted to know.

He started singing again, '*O, kala doria…*,' as if he had not heard her.

'We cannot eat so many. Two rupees worth would have been enough,' she insisted. 'I will give it to the boys when I go to play cricket,' he said, wrapping the leftover jalebis in the old newspaper in which they had been served.

On their way back, the children took a turn towards the ruins of the Budhhist stupa, which had been dug up the previous summer. Unknown to them, this had become the topic of animated discussion at archaeologists' conferences the world over. It was not yet open to the public, since loose bricks and broken pillars still lay scattered. Shamsie and Bheem crawled under the barbed wire with practised ease. They walked on one of the radial spokes of the brickwork which formed concentric circles around a round empty space. With chalks from their school bags, the two drew a large rectangle and, in the middle of the 2000-year-old prayer hall for Buddhist monks, played hopscotch which the children in Punjab called 'chhtaapu'. It was considered a girls' game, but Bheem played better than Shamsie, hopping nimbly from one square to the next.

The sun was going down fast, and it would soon be dark. They gathered their bags and crawled out under the fence without getting their uniforms nicked. The two walked towards their homes and, once inside the Vehra, Bheem started to sing even more freely, 'O, *kala doria*...'. He waved a cheery goodnight to Shamsie, who turned to ask again, 'Where did you get the money?'

'I earned it from cleaning Batta Master's house,' he said.

'But he does not pay you. You are supposed to do it for free,' she reminded him.

'I picked it up from under the pillow. So, what?' he said evasively, clearly wanting her gone.

'But that is stealing,' Shamsie persisted.

'Then he should not have made me wash Sunder's underwear.'

Shamsie nodded to indicate that she understood. With the key her father had given her, she opened the lock to their one-room home, which was four un-plastered brick walls, a row of logs supporting a brick and cement roof and a backdoor, beyond which was a lane that reeked perpetually of urine. A tin stove, little more than wicks dipped in a kerosene tank and covered with soot and food flecks, lay in a corner. On shelves made of wooden strips from empty fruit boxes stood small jars of salt, chillies, and rice. The jar of sugar was placed in an earthen bowl filled with water to prevent ants from getting at it. A tin can, which grocers bought ghee in from wholesalers, had been improvised with a cover and a wire loop to keep it closed. This was used to store wheat flour. Krishan slept on the jute cot with a striped durrie spread on it. For Shamsie, there was a straw mat and a thin quilt for a mattress. A moth-eaten closet, bought from a junk dealer, had been painted green and fixed into the wall.

After dinner, when Krishan went out to smoke and gossip with his friends, Shamsie looked inside the closet to see whether she had a clean uniform for the next day. Later, she dipped her hand into a hole in the wall behind the closet that she had dug with a knife. She carefully prised out the delicate bronze figure of a dancing woman, smaller than her hand, which she had found six months ago in a freshly ploughed field, long after the dig. The figure lay partly covered in earth, but Shamsie had known right away what it was. Even before the dig, for as long she could remember, she had been seeing a tall dancing girl in her dream, very much like the bronze figurine she found in the field. The bronze figure was real, something she could touch and feel, unlike the girl in her dream.

Two years ago, the dream had become more vivid and Shamsie had started walking in her sleep, following the young woman of her dream, who beckoned her. When brought back to bed by Krishan, she would mutter something about a dance hall. Krishan was amused at first, but panicked when it started happening every night. He took her to a *peer*, a Muslim faith-healer, on the other side of the canal. There, a young man of 20, with premature grey hair, muttered something in Shamsie's ear which made her tickle. He gave Krishan a clump of dried leaves to keep under Shamsie's pillow. It worked. The dream and the sleepwalking considerably lessened, and finally, stopped. Since the dreams stopped around the same time, Shamsie had found the bronze statue, in her mind, that was the reason for her restful nights. Shamsie had not told her father about her find, because he would have made her give it to the museum. That was what was required of those villagers who came across any such finds from the *khudai*, as the man on the rickshaw who had gone around the village had announced on a loudspeaker.

Shamsie kept the figure on a shelf and tried to mimic the pose in front of a broken mirror. With her thighs flared out and knees apart, right foot on the ground and left in the air, Shamsie rested her left forearm on a bent knee and the stretched the right, up and out, making sure to keep both arms aligned in a straight line.

Upon hearing Krishan's footsteps, she quickly hid back her forbidden treasure.

***

Bheem, on the other hand, did not go home as he did not have the key. His father was delayed again, and it was not yet time for his mother to be back. Comrade Ram was often late. He was a trade union leader, hence the 'Comrade'. He stayed back for 'gate meetings', an affable term for sloganeering against the owners for one reason or the other: a denied bonus, less payment for overtime, or the unjust firing of a comrade. Often, it was just a show of strength. 'We should not allow the weapon of protest to become blunt. So, we just meet at the gate after work and shout slogans till Bauji and his son's car has passed. Keeps them on their toes,' he had once told Bheem proudly.

Since he was locked out of his house, Bheem joined the group of boys playing cricket with a rubber ball and bat. The 'bat' had been picked up by one of the boys from a garbage dump in town. The handle was missing, but some nails and a whittled-down washing stick was all that was required to make a cricket bat sturdy enough for a rubber ball. Bheem was in a particularly attacking form that day, his boiling anger at the Granthi having returned. He hit the ball all over the place, even beyond the Vehra wall, which was a foul. When asked to give the bat to the next boy, he fought aggressively and came home with a bump on his forehead and a black eye.

'It is a matter of rules, jalebis or no jalebis,' somebody had tried to explain when he had turned to leave.

'Tripped in the dark while walking back,' he explained to Shamsie the next morning. He casually went on to ask her the usual wages that a maid from the Vehra got from a Jat household for doing chores. After Shamsie had accused him of stealing, he had decided to take from Batta's house just the exact money due to him. He could have asked his mother, but she had a knack for seeing through him, which made him wary. She was a stickler for the right and would have spanked him all over the Vehra, had she come to know about the stolen fiver. When Bheem was five, she had noticed that he preferred his left hand for writing. She coaxed, cajoled, and then twisted the fingers of his left hand, looking all the while at his face to know if she was hurting him too much. When that did not work, she got his left hand fixed in plaster through a compounder at the civil hospital whom she knew, and beat Bheem daily, till he could manage to write with his right hand. Never mind the result that Bheem was left with a bad handwriting and a right-left confusion for life. Every time he wanted to be sure about left from right, he had to look for the mole on his leg just above the ankle. The mole side was the right side and the other, the left.

Shamsie told him that her neighbour's wife, who was a cleaning and washing maid, got 150 rupees per month plus three meals. But why did he want to know? 'My cousin wants to shift from Jalandhar; the rents there are high,' Bheem replied.

Shamsie, of course, knew that he had no cousin. Since Bheem worked part time for two hours a day and did not receive any food, he fixed his own salary for work at Batta's house at 40 rupees a month. And out of the odd money lying around the house, he would pick exactly that much. Plus, one rupee for each time he found the undergarments of his classmate in the laundry. That, he thought, would satisfy his comrade father's sense of fair wages and dignity of labour.

It was around this time that an extreme left insurgency in far off Naxalbari in West Bengal caught the fancy of the state youth. Most of them were Dalit workers, but there were also some Jat students from families of poor farmers. Within weeks, it escalated into a violent class war. As the months went by, Comrade Ram would be picked up by the police at dawn every few weeks. Suspected of being a Naxalite or of having information about other Naxalite leaders, he would be beaten black and blue, and eventually released two or three days later. As the years went on, despite knowing fully well that he was a mere factory level sloganeer, Bheem's father would still be detained along with others who had at any time taken part in a labour unrest. This was a kind of rote cosmetic exercise for public consumption, whenever a rich man was murdered. This went on even years after the violent insurgency had been snuffed out through staged police encounters. Even when the police knew that the Naxalites had been dead for years and that the murder was not political, the men would be kept in jail for a week or two till the real culprits were found. At these times, it was Bheem who carried food and painkillers to the police station every day. He would miss the first few periods at school on those days, but would reach before the final bell, which was when school attendance was marked. He made sure to be on time for his cleaning and washing duties at Batta's house. It was around then that Bheem transitioned from singing peppy folk tunes to lyrics of defiance. His adolescent anger found an outlet in a spring of rousing songs.

Four

This was around the same time that my own life had started going to seed. I had gotten divorced a year earlier. Reema had left on the day of the last court hearing, to join her old job in England. She still called about mundane issues of bank accounts, certificates from the medical council, and the like. I had to go to Chandigarh for such tasks. Money was never an issue between us. She felt secure with what she got, and I just did not care. There was no custody battle since there were no children. And given the distance between us now, things were cordial.

I had been diagnosed with clinical depression many years ago. To be fair to Reema, this one was not on her. My first bout of depression had been during one of the long and dark British winters, long before I met her. But when we met, I had been fine for years. The second time was three years after we had been married. While our relationship was stretched taut due to many other reasons, some of her making and some mine, my depression was the final straw, and things had then crumbled fast between us. Living with a depressed person is one of the most draining experiences anyone can be subjected to, I was told by my psychiatrist. Going quiet and irritable on a partner can kill a relationship quicker than infidelity, he had gone on.

I eventually recovered after treatment, but by then, our marriage was a train wreck. In fact, I was the one who had suggested divorce. Friends, who thought my living like a recluse on a dusty hillock on the far bank of a river was because of my divorce, were wrong. I was always a recluse and Reema did say once that she had found my aloofness mysterious and sexy. What depression did, however, was to make a proper illness out of a mere temperament. With Reema's departure, I was free to follow my so-called mind and live where I pleased.

The concept of cause and effect is anyway overrated. After a while, it is impossible to separate one from the other since the effect can become the cause leading to further effects, and so it goes on...till, in the end, all you have is a ball of entangled wool of cause and effect. But it is yours to bump against the wall of the rest of your life.

After Reema left, I sold our Chandigarh house, which doubled as a clinic. Patients bothered me, because I knew I was short-changing them. While seeing patients, my mind would be wandering all over the place. I would remember the look on my father's face eons back, when on a dark rainy day in Amritsar, in a clinic through the window of which one could make out the dome of the Golden Temple, he was told by a psychiatrist that my mother had depression. While checking a patient's blood pressure, I would recall the sudden exasperation on his face. He considered it a personal slur and shot back, 'What is she depressed about? We have our own house, a car, and a lovely boy.' I would recall how he had shoved me forward, like a piece of evidence, as if the eight-year-old me was immunity against clinical depression. With those thoughts in my mind, by the time I reached the diastolic blood pressure of my patient, I would have forgotten the systolic. Patients sensed that I was absent-minded. Patients know more about their doctors than they let on. Behaviour out of the ordinary makes them edgy. To assuage their panic, patients sometimes ask questions. Mine did, and they did not like the answers. They did not feel at ease in the hands of a doctor who could not keep his own life together.

***

There was this small house on the beaten down road along the bank of Satluj, miles away from any city, or for that matter, from any village. For me, the good part was that it was far from Chandigarh. The house was suggested by the property agent who had sold our Chandigarh house, and who by then knew of my idiosyncrasies.

The actual river remained far away most of the year. Between the water edge and the raised riverbank, on which the lone house stood, was a wide stretch of tall 'elephant grass' and wild bush teaming with jackals, snakes, and scorpions. At night, the racket of crickets from the dense shrubbery made sleep difficult. During monsoon, the river would swell, and water would be just 50 yards away. The road ran parallel to the river bank for 15 km. At the end of the road downstream was a pontoon bridge, built and managed by the Indian Army, but open to all. They had a unit stationed there to train soldiers for riverine battles. The trainees came in batches from other parts of the country. Another kilometre downstream, the four-lane Grand Trunk Road, also called National Highway 1, crossed the river on a long, majestic bridge, probably one of the busiest bridges in the country. Long trucks, some with 12 wheels bearing the legend 'From Kashmir to Kanyakumari, India is one', trundled across the bridge at all hours. It was the paramilitary, and not the state police, which guarded it those days.

On most nights, several fires could be seen along the river in the middle of the wild bush on my side of the river, because the other side was the city side, and these were bootleggers distilling hooch. On some nights, I would be woken up by stray dogs barking relentlessly and police jeeps racing up and down the road, after which, fires would not light up for many days. The dogs were in hundreds and were fed by the bootleggers. During the day, they slept at the distilleries, and at night, ran along the road, acting as lookouts. If there was a police jeep, the dogs would kick up a racket and the bootleggers would douse their fires and scamper away in the dark.

There was a veranda at the back on the ground floor of the house, and a balcony above it, both facing the river. The rest of the house was a large room with windows opening towards the road, and a kitchen and a room on the upper floor. There were no neighbours for miles. The property agent said that it was built by a Britisher as a hunting lodge when the river side was a dense forest, teeming with wild life. The deer would come to the river to drink water, and apparently, to be shot at, but that could have been just a property agent's yarn. However, it was clear that nobody had lived there for many years. Once the cobwebs were cleared, one could see the floor was covered with years of dust, and not just the paint, the plaster too had come off the walls. I was promised it would be repaired and repainted if I was willing to buy and paid an advance. I did as told, so wrung out I was of any feeling this way or that, as far as the house was concerned. I am sure if the property agent had taken me to another house in the thick of the city I would have still signed the papers, as long as it was far from Chandigarh. I was running away from my past and hundred kilometres was alright as a start.

I did not buy any furniture for the ground floor. My car, a 10-year-old Fiat, remained parked inside the gate. I stayed on the first floor and cooked for myself, something I had learnt out of necessity when I was in England for my fellowship. I did not put up a name plate since patients were one thing I was running from. It must have been the milkman who told people I was a doctor, because a trickle of people with coughs and fevers started showing up a couple of weeks after I moved in. They must have sensed my utter lack of interest in them and the trickle remained just that. But it did make me bring down out of politeness two chairs and a table from upstairs. I had high blood pressure myself and kept a blood pressure apparatus and a stethoscope at home. These I started using for the patients. And the few patients that I had took liberty to climb up the stairs looking for me, if I was not in the clinic downstairs.

Like Shamsie that day, who was feeling parched because of her medicines. I gave her water and we climbed down the spiral staircase made of rusted iron, which moved and creaked when in use. It had a view of the river, even of the far bank and it was windy on the stairs most times. She had come to ask if the medicines could have delayed her periods. That also explained why she had come alone. She looked more curious than worried. It was when I told her it was unlikely that she told me, in her detached manner, that she had been staying with Bheem whenever she went to the village. But they took precautions, the 16-year-old wanted me to know.

Before she could go to a laboratory for a test in the city, which she was willing to go without showing any hesitation, she got her periods, and that was that. She had called to inform me. 'I thought you might worry.'

She met me another time, several months later, when her school finished. She had brought a gift. It was a bottle of Peter Scot whiskey, which she carried unselfconsciously. Bheem's cousin, a truck driver in Australia, had brought it, she said. She must have bought it herself, because Peter Scot was an Indian whiskey, and as I came to know later, Bheem had no cousin in Australia or anywhere else.

Before going, she asked some more questions about her illness, like although she would be taking medicines regularly, what if she still got another fit. I explained that it did happen sometimes, and if it did, she should consult the nearest doctor and let me know on the phone. By then, I knew that she was going away for some time. The gift, the questions—all pointed to that. But I did not ask, and she did not tell. But she did tell me something else. That when she got the fit, just before passing out, she had the same vision as she had when she sleepwalked. She was curious if there was a connection between epilepsy and sleep walking in her case and why was she 'seeing' a dancing girl beckoning her in both.

'She looks like this,' she said taking out of her trousers' pocket an exquisite bronze statue of a girl in a stunning dance pose. 'I brought it to show you.' And then went on to tell me the story of her find.

When I had gathered myself after seeing the sublimely beautiful bronze figure, which I knew would be worth a lot of money in the right hands and knew that her carrying it around was probably illegal, I tried to answer her question as simply as I could. Maybe, it was just that as a small child, 'khudai' was all she heard about, and that stayed in her mind. And since she had found the statue, she was so fascinated by it that she wanted to emulate it—that was probably why she had joined a school which had a dance teacher. And I told her I did not know for sure; I was just guessing.

Epilepsy is not a very predictable illness I said, and childhood memories can be deceptive. Also, one remembers things the way one wants to. There was a mocking smile on her lips. 'Or maybe I was there three thousand years back,' she said laughing as I saw her out. I noticed, when she laughed, her eyes danced and dimples came up on the dusky cheeks.

Five

What Master Batta on that rain-swept day was trying to teach his young students with three progressively smaller maps of the state, maps which Shamsie could not properly see because of Bheem's head blocking her view was probably something like this:

The original Punjab (let us call it P-1) was divided in 1947 at the time of the Partition of India. Pakistan got the bigger chunk and the rest, say P-2, became the Indian Punjab. This, as historians would tell us, also contained the future states of Haryana and Himachal Pradesh. Shimla was the capital till 1960, while a new capital for P-2 designed by a French architect was being built. The location of that capital was based on pragmatic considerations that it would be roughly central for all the areas in P-2, which extended from the Himalayas in the north to the dusty plains bordering Delhi in the south.

However, barely six years after the P-2 government had moved into its new capital, Chandigarh, it was time for another split.

The second split was self-inflicted. Some Sikh leaders wanted a state of their own. Since they could not have asked for a religion-based state in a secular country, they used the pretext of language. They projected themselves as leaders of all Punjabis, which they were not. Nor were they leaders of all Sikhs for that matter. But stridently vociferous they certainly were. There were protests and hunger strikes. They stopped trains, burnt buses, and held seminars in the gleaming conference rooms of their new capital with maps of P-2 and pointed at the hills in the north and the area around Delhi in the south, and asked, 'Why are those people with us? They do not speak Punjabi, do they?'

It was all very confusing for the common people. Here were their leaders burning buses, because their state was too big and wanted it to be truncated at both ends. The central government was happy to oblige. They removed the non-Punjabi speaking areas and even some Punjabi speaking ones from P-2. When asked, they explained that they did not want to take a chance. You wanted small. Here it is. Even smaller. Enjoy.

Protesters, with many of them being old men in blue turbans, had their prestige on line and were tired. They were in no mood to protest all over again, on the ground, 'We wanted small. But not this small!'

All the hill districts, and even some plains, were transferred to the new state of Himachal Pradesh and what was south P-2 became Haryana. Chandigarh, the new capital, too was taken away from P-2 and appropriated by the central government for itself. It graciously allowed both P-2 and Haryana to use the city as their capital, but only as guests of the central government, not as owners of the city.

The leftover rump (let us call it P-3), the current Punjab at the time of this story, had its capital not just outside the boundaries of P-3, but also under another government. A capital in exile became the seat of a government in exile of P-3.

One would have thought that the politicians and bureaucrats of P-3 would have resented at least the inconvenience caused to them if not to the people of P-3. That they would have been upset at this freak arrangement where they had to live away from the people they loved and who loved them back, look at the numbers of votes they gave them. And while the problems facing the state of P-3 had their epicentre at one end of the state, they, the solution, were beyond the other end. And their primary constituents, the farmers who jauntily drove their tractor trolleys on the village and city roads of P-3, could not enter their own capital, because the central government did not allow trolleys on its roads.

On the contrary, both the politicians and the officers governing the state realized the many benefits of living as guests at public expense in a modern city, without the headache of having to govern it. Chandigarh had some of the best hospitals, schools, and universities in the country. It had a modern airport and a slew of fast trains to Delhi and beyond. It did not matter if there was no direct train track to any part of P-3. Who needed trains when chauffeured cars with outriders on jeeps were there for routine inspections of P-3 and helicopters for urgent ones?

Any objection on the grounds of practicality of the arrangement was met with the rejoinder that if the British could govern the whole of India so well from Shimla tucked away in a remote hilly corner, during the long Indian summers, why could the government in exile not govern a state right there? While saying 'right there', the speaker would point with his thumb backwards, his fist closed over his shoulder as if P-3 was the backyard of Chandigarh. The gentleman in beige tweed would then take a sip from his Earl Grey tea and explain further to the batch of young administrative trainees from the Mussoorie academy, 'It is important to be rational in administration and for that, one needs to be objective, which in turn needs some degree of detachment, which requires distance. When you are part of an entity, you cannot be entirely rational about it. Emotions interfere. To be completely analytical about an issue you must be situated outside that problem. The government in exile is an experiment in rational administration for the betterment of the lives of people of P-3. The need to be detached to perform one's duty, one's dharma also finds prominent mention in Shrimad Bhagavad Gita and is in line with our ancient heritage and its philosophical moorings, he would elaborate. The wives were happy too. Chandigarh lay at the foot of hills and just a two-hour-drive from some salubrious mountain resorts. A top-notch residential school, the alumni of which included central ministers, army generals and business leaders, lay cradled among low hills just an hour away and parents had the luxury of meeting their children every other Sunday. On the golf courses on weekends and in the officers' club on weekdays, they decried the pollution, the power cuts, the gang wars, and the dilapidated doctor-less hospitals of P-3, forgetting over time that they were the ones responsible for its governance. They became too detached even by the standards of the Bhagavad Gita. Ministers and the officers and their wives at the kitties rued the situation in P-3 and agreed, 'Certainly not a place to live.'

'Or to die,' the retired ones would add. And they kept their word too. No minister or officer of the government in exile of the state of P-3, worth his salt, settled in P-3 after retirement or died there.

And then, there were the Kakas. The Kakas of Chandigarh. There were some pre-requisites before you could be called that. You had to be from a Jat Sikh family, but not any Jat Sikh family. A Jat family which owned at least 200 acres of land in P-3, land ceiling law or no land ceiling law. And a large house in one of the posh sectors of Chandigarh, the ones with a single digit number. And a working knowledge of golf for men, because a golf course was where the mornings were spent. For the rest of the time, they wore well-starched white kurta-churidars and did nothing. The Kakas of Chandigarh had made an art out of doing nothing. The clan was fiercely endogamous, and hence, intricately inter-related. They were also highly political. Almost all the chief ministers and a good majority of ministers came from this stock.

Since it seemed unseemly that for decades upon decades, the reins of the government were held uninterruptedly by members of a single elite clan, they had divided themselves for appearance's sake into two blocks and ruled alternately. In addition to their white kurta churidars, one group wore blue turbans and the other any colour but blue. Also, the men of one group used alcohol and the other opium, so that one could not be mistaken for the other.

Six

An outlandish con that Punjabis have been able to sell to the rest of India and the world at large is that the state of P-3 has five rivers. Like a sleigh of hand, they would use the original name of P-1.

'See, the word "Punjab" comes from "punj" plus "aab". "Punj" is five and "aab" is water, which means rivers. Right? Right. So, the land of five rivers it is.'

What P-3 has is two rivers and a half. There is Satluj out there, behind my house. Its tributary, Beas, comes crashing down the steep hills and meets it before the river enters Pakistan on its westward journey. The river Ravi does not pass through P-3. It divides it from the hilly states of Jammu and Kashmir, and Himachal Pradesh and P-3 can claim one bank at the most. So, two and a half it is. Five is what P-1 had before Partition, with Jhelum, Chenab, Ravi, Beas, and Satluj.

And in the one of those two and a half rivers of P-3, dead bodies started turning up the summer after I moved into that house. The first one, I saw one morning, when I was on the terrace, smoking. I had not smoked for over 10 years, and then, suddenly one afternoon, I was driving on the potholed road to the shanty row of shops next to the pontoon bridge. The brand I had quit in England had not reached here, so I bought what the woman at the stall said the Army officers smoked, which was Wills Navy Cut.

I had seen more dead bodies in my first two years in England than most doctors see in a lifetime. To pad up the subsistence money that my fellowship paid, I did locum duties in Forensic Pathology on weekends and on holidays, assisting in autopsies on dead bodies of murder victims.

This one was a young man, as were all the subsequent ones I would see from my terrace. The body was floating flat with face up to the sky, with hands and feet thrown out in gay abandon, and the long hair floating in tow. The blue kurta and the white pyjama had been rolled up by waves. Even from that far, I could make out that the man had been shot in the head from close range from the size of the hole on his forehead, which no doubt appeared even bigger from that distance because of the gun powder ring around it.

Like I said, there were more dead bodies to come. Not just in the river, but also on the roads, in trains, at city crossings, even falling from the skies out of planes. Happily, drunk, dancing men and women in a marriage procession would turn into dead bodies without a notice as would flocks of morning walkers in parks across the state.

Everybody called it the 'Punjab Problem', as if it were a stubborn crossword puzzle refusing to be solved and not a ruthlessly violent terrorist insurgency. There were several versions of how it had started, but the common denominators included a turbaned 'Dandy' (who dressed in white and sported a rose to look like Nehru), 'Durga' (who, in the end was slain by the demons), and a fiery 'Priest' bristling with a long beard and automatic weapons. The Dandy had lost the Chief Ministership of P-3 after a bitterly fought fair and square election and wanted revenge. He fell crying at Durga's feet, rose and all, and convinced her to put the Priest up as a counterweight to his bête noire, the new chief minister and was encouraged to kill some people ostensibly in the service of Sikh faith to gain currency. He came to love doing that. Particularly after followers of the faith who lived abroad applauded and sent hotshot journalists of international magazines for interviews and photographs, which made the Priest famous. Supposed to be Durga's man, but now puffed up, he rebelled, and started a war to get a country of his own, another land of the pure, this time for the Sikhs—the genie which refused to go back into the bottle, a Frankenstein gone rogue.

Newspapers were not delivered where I lived. There was a telephone connected to a rural exchange, which seldom worked. I did have a transistor radio, but the radio stations those days were government run and purveyed a staid commentary of the bloodletting sweeping the state. The morning news was a stark body count of those who had died overnight. The milkman said that in his father's opinion, another Partition would happen soon, since the last time dead bodies flowed in the Satluj, the country broke in two.

The milkman was a one-armed clean-shaven Sikh, Jeet. He had a piece of advice for me, which he bandied around every other day. Leave this house and go to a city. You hardly see any patients anyway. You keep moping and smoking a whole lot of cigarettes, you can do that as well in the city. The Sikh in him disapproved of my smoking, but this was different.

'I swear by Baba Nanak, I cannot wrap my head around your being here in the first place.' He looked very perplexed as he said it.

'Not that the city is any guarantee for a long life with your cigarettes and all that. But here! A Hindu, in a lonely house on the riverbank, is a sitting duck. Why would Sikh terrorists fighting for a country only for the Sikhs spare you? Not that being a Sikh is any guarantee,' he added wistfully.

Already neck deep in a morass of deadening inertia, what I gathered was that there were no guarantees, so why bother.

But Jeet was relentless and came up with a fresh argument every few days: 'This is not even a proper road. If something happens to you, nobody will come to know till I come next morning.'

'How does it matter to a dead me when I am found?' I asked. That further upset him. Whenever he was agitated, the stump of his right arm, which he would be trying to point in my direction, moved rapidly up and down.

The amputation was the result of his pushing fodder into a chopping machine when he was 17. Just then, the buffalo had pulled its peg out and ran away, peg, chain, and all. His father hollered. Distracted, Jeet forgot to stop pushing the fodder and the sharp and strong blade made a clean cut through his arm. Neighbours gathered and then ran around to collect whatever ice was frozen in all the three refrigerators of the village, which was not much since electricity had been intermittent. Jeet and his hand packed in some ice cubes were taken to the city on a motorcycle, which the sarpanch had lent his father. The doctors at the medical college managed to stitch the wayward body part back to its place, but it turned blue in a few hours and in the morning had to be amputated by the same surgeon who had spent four hours stitching it the previous night.

'Too little ice,' he explained.

'Too little ice,' the nurse rued.

'Too little ice,' rued the orderly and the sweeper, who got tips when hands stayed pink.

'At least, buy a gun. I can talk to my cousin. He is a big shot in the DC office. He can get you a license.'

'What a sure way of getting killed, thank you very much,' I replied. 'That would be inviting the "Boys" who would travel miles on their motorcycles just to snatch the gun for their own use.'

'Boys' was what everybody called them, since most of them were frightfully young. In the beginning, the newspapers called them terrorists, till three sub-editors of English, Hindi, and Punjabi dailies were kidnapped and, days later, found roughed up and tied to an electricity pole one morning, at the city crossing. They were not terrorists but warriors in a religious war, the statement in respective languages pinned to the sub-editor's shirt collars explained. The newspapers by an unwritten agreement settled on 'militants'. The 'Boys', however, was what they continued to be called by the people.

Every few weeks, clean-shaven men travelling in night buses got pulled out, lined up on the roadside, and shot. The number of bearded men in P-3 suddenly grew. And Hindu men learnt how to tie turbans. The Boys caught on fast and started asking the men travelling in night buses to recite verses from Gurbani to separate grain from the chaff. They ran into a problem right away. Many Sikhs, the younger ones particularly, did not know Gurbani either.

Dark humour took over. It seems, one Boy told another, 'I wish they were circumcized. We could just pull the trousers down and decide like they did at the time of Partition. Those guys had it so easy.'

And there was this one that Jeet told me. A bus is stopped on a deserted road. Men, who are clean-shaven, are asked to get off and stand in a queue. The leader tells his men to paint their faces black. Men down the line become impatient and jostle to get their faces painted out of turn. The leader shouts at them, 'Why are you so eager? One would think laddoos are being distributed.'

The man at the end of the queue replied, 'Sir, if the paint finishes, you will shoot the rest of us... Ha, ha, ha.'

For me, the war reached my door in the form of dead dogs. A whole lot of them in fact. Around midnight, I heard some shooting. Half asleep, I wondered if this was a relapse of my hallucinations. There were short staccato bursts one associates with automatic weapons, interspersed with long periods of silence. Seemed to be far, but getting closer. Then some pistol shots were fired on the road right outside my window, followed by yelping sounds. There were sounds of motorcycles driving away. I slept fitfully till daybreak. When I opened the window, two stray dogs lay dead in the middle of the road below. I came down to see another one lying in the bush not far away, the trail of dried blood coming down the slope and crossing the road all the way. When I looked up and down the road, there were dead dogs and streaks of blood crossing the road like some gory road markings as far as I could see. My first thought was that the police had killed the dogs, so they could surprise the bootleggers. But the police did not have bullets to spare. They would have just poisoned the dogs.

Jeet got down from his cycle and told me all the dogs in the nearby villages had also been shot dead during the night. And it had nothing to do with bootleggers. It was the Boys who had gone around the villages during the night, shooting all the strays. Posters were found on walls ordering villagers to poison their pet dogs. Otherwise, the Boys would come back and do the job. And shoot the owners too. It seemed the dogs gave away the Boys' movements at night. People were now planning to put the dogs to sleep. It had to be done when children were away at school. The villagers spent the whole day burying dead dogs, Jeet told me the following morning. Each village buried their dogs in two mass graves, one for the pets near the gurudwara, and the other for the strays outside the village. That was the least they could do for their pets, they felt.

Seven

The terrorists were younger and fitter, better trained, much better equipped, and far more motivated than the police. Money came from some of the Punjabi diaspora in Great Britain and Canada (hereafter called Grenada in the service of brevity, knowing well that Grenada is an entirely different country), with which hardware was bought from across the border from a friendly neighbourhood establishment, who were happy to throw in free training. Every assassination of a high-profile leader or a train blast or a massacre in a park left the clueless police even more demoralized, and thus, even less effective. In public perception, the Boys attained magical, even supernatural, qualities. They came, they killed, they vanished.

Panic bells went off. High profile parleys were held by the government-in-exile in the capital-in-exile, one of which went on until dawn, when hazy outlines of the Shivalik hills could be made out in the north through the chinks in curtains of the governor's house. Conclusions had been reached, and security policies overhauled.

There is a popular saying in Hindi that if frozen ghee cannot be taken out of the can with a straight finger, one should use a crooked finger. In keeping with this wisdom, cities and villages across P-3 witnessed an overnight transferring out of all police officers with straight fingers. They were posted at offices in the capital-in-exile, in departments like Information Technology, Police Housing, Human Resource Development, and VIP security. Meanwhile, officers with crooked fingers were posted on operational duty at police stations and district headquarters of P-3, to take out the proverbial ghee from the can. This swap did not help as far as the death count was concerned, but it did make the battle more even for a while, slowing down the slide into total anarchy.

The road in front of my house, 9 km ahead, branched off to the right before it ended at the pontoon bridge. After 2 km, this lane disappeared into the back door of the Gurukul. Gurukul, which means a seminary, a place of teaching and learning, was sprawled over a hundred acres.

A place of teaching indeed it was. The Gurukul was where the rookie policemen were trained in techniques of modern policing. Fingerprints, DNA analysis, lie detection, and the like. Distinguished professors from renowned universities across the country came to lecture trainees about scientific methods of interrogation, intricacies of the criminal mind, and sociocultural factors that bred criminality and public disorder. The Gurukul attracted trainees even from some African countries.

The 2 km-long road, which led to the rear entrance of the Gurukul, had on both sides a tall fence of crisscross steel wire. Farmers with fields on either side could not use that road. Instead, they had to walk a long winding route to work in their own fields. That too, only after they had been thoroughly searched for weapons. They swore that the road was strictly one way, because the jeeps that went towards the Gurukul and their male occupants (they were all young men) were never seen coming back. It was as if they had been gobbled up by the Gurukul or had disappeared into thin air. Gradually, the road came to be known as 'Gaayab Sarak' or 'The Vanishing Road'. The road, of course, did not vanish. Just the men.

The rear part of the Gurukul had an elegant annex-like building, which, from the outside, looked like a well-funded library. It had wide glass doors and windows giving the appearance of absolute transparency. The glass, however, if you could come close, was one way and soundproof. This building, called simply the 'Gym', had not always been as posh as this. During the Naxalite insurgency, it was a decrepit ruin, a leftover stable from some earlier times, which served as an interrogation centre. That the leftist militancy had been effectively crushed in less than three years was to a great extent due to the role played by Gaayab Sarak and the Gym. A period less than a decade separated the Naxal insurgency from the current one. This respite was ample time for the Gym to be renovated. These were also the heydays of the agricultural revolution, and the government and the people too had a lot of money. The Gym now housed state-of-the-art equipment to coax information out of reluctant clients, while the glass and the rows of potted plants at the entrance continued adding to the softness of the façade. The Gym was the only part of the Gurukul out of bounds for trainees. And it was controlled directly from the headquarters in the capital in exile, not by the director of the Gurukul.

The Gurukul itself was more like a bustling township. It boasted of several lecture halls, an auditorium, a modern office complex and residential buildings around the centre piece of an 18-holed golf course. Between the Gym and the main campus was a four-acre enclosure, surrounded by a barbed fence. Hundreds of police dogs, some of whom stayed permanently, and some, who came for training from countries as far off as Zimbabwe, were caged here.

The golf course and the swimming pool were open to some select members of the public. These were 'who is who' of the city, which was a 20-minute drive across the river, by the swank boulevard starting from the front entrance of the Gurukul. The road had no official name, but villagers called it the 'Zaahir Sarak' or the 'Visible Road'. The jeeps which went in through the Gayab Sarak emerged on the Zaahir Sarak. They had by then dropped their passengers at the Gym and were now going back to the countryside to pick up more fare.

Eight

The rain had been relentless for four days now, and the entire expanse of elephant grass was under swirling waters. Just the spiny tips showed at some places. The familiar cacophony of crickets at night had gone eerily quiet. The low clouds, the high waves, the electricity blackout, and the dead telephone had all shrunk my small world even further. Jeet, too, had not come for four days. Not that I cared about any of it. My only concern was that since the road in front of my house was under two feet of water and the car had a low ground clearance, my monthly trip to the city had been delayed. I had finished my medicines and had hardly slept for several days.

The ritual of going to the city every month to see my psychiatrist, buy groceries, and get the Fiat serviced and refilled was a necessary chore. I considered my visits to my psychiatrist as mundane a task as servicing my Fiat, without which, both the car and I, would stutter and stop. But I could not go any day I wanted to. Dr Mustafa, who worked in the medical college run by Christian missionaries, had his OPD only on Mondays and Fridays, and I had to schedule my trip accordingly. Not that it mattered to me. The few patients I saw came any day of the week at any time of the day, whenever I was home. There was no guarantee of when I would be home. But my patients knew I hardly went out. They could call on the phone, whenever it worked, but none of my patients had a telephone.

That I looked at my consultations with Dr Mustafa as a burdensome task was pointed out by him. 'I do not expect you to be gung-ho about it, or about anything else for that matter. That is what depression is. It is the nature of the beast,' he said that morning.

He asked about my sleep, whether my mood changed with the time of day and about any hallucinations. Since we were both doctors, we often lapsed into technical terms out of habit, although that is not the best practice. I told him about the gun shots I kept hearing at night ever since the stray dogs' massacre night. He vaguely knew where I lived, since he had been born in the village next to the school, just a kilometre from the river. As it turned out, Dr Mustafa was a Christian; his father having bartered his religion for his son's education. All this I had learnt from his plump and chirpy secretary—a practising nun, complete with a tunic, with a cross and beads hanging from her belt, and a Jesus on the wall above her head.

'I have stopped putting any diagnostic premium on these symptoms of gunfire sounds, ever since all of this started,' said he, sweeping his hand in the general direction of the outside world, as if to explain what he meant by 'all of this'. I insisted that the gunfire sounds that I heard were real and not hallucinations.

'Reality is pretty psychotic these days,' he said. He had been trained in Britain and still had the accent and some of the wry wit.

Then he surprised me by baring *his* mind to me by talking about his diagnostic quandaries. I was sure it would have been described as unethical somewhere on the stiff pages of a Medical Council manual. 'You are a doctor, and you know that we psychiatrists do not have any investigation to diagnose a mental illness. We have no thermometre to calibrate the degree of psychosis. All we have is a clinical assessment of whether the patient has lost contact with reality. But what does one do when reality itself has lost contact with reality; you know, what I mean?' He was pleading and was desperate to be understood, and of course, I did understand. But to see one's doctor confused about the basics of his learning is an unnerving feeling, and it must have shown on my face.

'No, no, it has nothing to do with you. Your diagnosis was established way back. In better times. We are safe there.'

'But imagine if you had come to me today,' he continued. After looking at my morose face, he changed the line of conversation a little bit. 'Alright; not you. Imagine if some other patient had come to me for the first time today, and said he felt anxious, had palpitations, and worried that he might die whenever he goes out. Earlier, I would have diagnosed him with Panic Disorder and Agoraphobia, prescribed him medication and reassured him. I would have told him he could not die out of the blue, when he had no physical illness.'

Dr Mustafa wore a dark suit with a bow tie, whatever the weather. In summers, he took off the jacket and hung it across the back of his chair. The air conditioner was on, but there were beads of sweat on his forehead. He was a tall, dark, bulky man with a presence. But that day, he looked helpless as a child as he tried to explain, 'Now, I cannot do it. Panic Disorder would sound so much of a fraud, because these days, perfectly healthy people go out for a walk in a park and die. Totally out of the blue! Without having any illness!'

Our roles had been reversed, and of course, I was not up to the task. I felt in a way short-changed. Too much was being expected from me. I was not only not a psychiatrist, but also a psychiatric patient myself.

'Try to understand. Before this, if a patient said that he feared he would be taken away by the police, I would tell him that he was paranoid. That there was no reason to worry since he had done nothing wrong. Now I cannot do that, because the police is in fact taking away people, even those who have done no wrong. So, tell me, what do I tell him?' he wondered.

Looking more and more like the captain of a boat who had lost his compass on a cloudy night, he asked me in a plaintive tone, 'So, how do I work? Advise me. You are a doctor too.'

He had me so rattled, I told him that as much as I understood his rudderless plight, would he please just repeat my prescription if no changes were required. I wanted to go before the Ramgarhia mechanic, who was servicing my Fiat, closed his garage for lunch.

But Dr Mustafa had more to say, 'It is not for me to suggest life choices to you. But, have you considered moving back to a city? You can even see patients yourself now that you are better.'

'Why does everyone want me to move? You are right, it is not for you to suggest,' I said, more testily than I intended to. 'I like it here. Looking back, I have always preferred to live alone. I was the happiest when living on my own for a year in a Welsh village.'

'Who said anything about not living alone? You can live alone in a city. There are people who do that. As far as I know, nobody in the city is hiding in a dark street waiting to snatch your singlehood from you. Besides, where you live is not a Welsh village. It is not even a village for God's sake.' He looked at the door to make sure Sister Josephine had not heard him swearing. 'It is wilderness. Chances of your getting shot like those dogs are rather high. Statistically significant, I would say.'

'So, you are now worried about me. Isn't that called counter transference? And isn't getting attached to a patient unethical?' I liked to draw him out occasionally. Plus, I was irritated at being hounded by questions about relocation, when most days, I did not feel like going out to buy cigarettes.

You should be nice to him in his vulnerable time, I told myself. After all, he just lost his compass, his North Star, the only thermometre he had, reality.

'I might think about it.' I said, and was happy to get away. But on my way out, I did look up at the Jesus on the wall and hoped he showed light to Dr Mustafa. Whatever had been the motives of his father becoming a Christian, Dr Mustafa was a good Christian by all accounts.

***

When I returned from the city, I saw a scooter inside the gate of my house, which I kept unlocked during the day. An old Vespa from the times it was Vespa, not Bajaj, was parked in the slushy ground outside the clinic door which was ajar. Two people sat on a bench with their backs to the door. They turned around and it was apparently a young couple. The man wore a shiny safari suit, which must have been stifling in the humidity—was my first thought. As my eyes got used to the darkness, I recognized the tall dark girl as Shamsie. She asked if I remembered her. She would have been about 19, but looked an elegant grown up woman in the grey sari with maroon border, a grey blouse, and a rather outsized bindi. And a beads' necklace and dangling silver earrings. In better times, Reema had joked about my observational skills, when it came to women's fashion. 'For a shy introvert man, you have a sharp eye for women's clothing,' she had said after I described a girl at a farmers' market in Cardiff, from whom I had just bought some apples at a bargain price. Reema wanted to go back and buy more of the same and I had, it seems, provided an accurate description.

The man next to Shamsie turned out to be Bheem. A stocky youngster with short hair who looked like an athletic plain-clothes cop, he was a shade fairer and an inch shorter than Shamsie. I remembered her telling me about her childhood friend, who was later her beau. Bheem looked confident and relaxed, despite the humidity and the terrycot safari suit. In comparison, it was Shamsie who was fidgety. She wanted to know if she should stop taking the medicine for epilepsy I had started her on, since she had heard the course was for three years. She did not have the prescription, but I remembered the medicines, which were a standard combination.

They had been in Bombay for the last two years. She had joined a dance school run by an aging choreographer, while Bheem worked as a bouncer in a dance bar. Those were the best days of their lives, she said. I reminded her she was just 19. But she was childlike, wide-eyed about the Elephanta Caves, the foreigners at the Gateway of India, the fast locals, the Ganesh, and the Govinda. She spoke fast, with wonder in her eyes and a guileless presumption that I could not have possibly heard of such a magical place, and looking at the wonderment on her face, I let her go on.

Bheem knew somebody, who knew somebody who worked as a bouncer in one of the hundred odd dance bars in Bombay. Bouncers doubled as waiters and kept an eye on clients, who sometimes tried to grab a dancer. What was allowed was a light touch while passing a currency note to the dancer. What was encouraged was 'scratching', in which, a tipsy man would peel off notes over a girl's head, Shamsie went on. This I had never heard of. The waiters were charged with the responsibility of escorting out men who crossed a line. They were also to hover and make sure the girls did not cheat management, by making a direct appointment with clients for after hours.

The dance itself, Shamsie added, was a shame where all that the women had to do was sway their body. The real dance, she said, was what they taught at the Nritya Academy. She had trained there for six months, the fee for which had come from selling her one-room village house. The academy was on the fourth floor of a building, which had no lift. The students were all small-town girls wanting to get into the movies. Mornings were for students and afternoons for families who wanted to learn choreographed steps in preparation for a family wedding. The walls of the reception area stood adorned with photos of famous producers and talent spotters visiting the dance academy for placements. The pictures, Shamsie found out later, were fake.

The two shared with another couple a two-roomed flat above the dance bar. After completing her course, Shamsie started to do the rounds of studios and offices in back alleys. She looked for bit roles, clutching her profile album, which had consumed the leftover money she had. She soon found that there were several ifs on that road. Starting with *if* the man sitting at the table opposite her was a real casting director. *If* the posters on the office wall were of an actual movie. And an all-too-often refrain she heard from casting directors was: 'If only you weren't so dark...'. She discovered after a long frustrating year that sleeping with the assistant producer was necessary, but not sufficient, to be cast even as a maid to the heroine. She said this plainly, without any anger or bitterness. As if she accepted the situation for what it was, without necessarily judging it. 'I did not want to do that. Not for those roles, I mean. For the heroine's role, I might have,' she said smilingly, glancing at Bheem.

They had returned about a month ago and were living in Bheem's room in the Vehra.

'No seizure?' I asked her.

'None.'

'Visions? Sleepwalking? Dancing girls from ancient times?' I asked as if jokingly, but it was important to know before deciding if the treatment could be stopped.

'Not even once,' she assured me.

I told her she could taper off the medicines over three months. Much later, she said she had lied to me about the visions, which she continued to have occasionally. Since the medicines had not stopped the visions, she had decided those were not connected to her illness, and so, not my domain. Maybe they were a connection to a previous life, she had thought at that time. After all, she had been seeing the visions ever since she was small and then she had found the bronze statue.

'Those did not bother me. In fact, I looked forward to the visions and Bheem had become used to my sleepwalking, and he would just nudge me back to my bed. I thought the visions had a purpose, something to do with my dancing,' she had told me, blowing a perfect circle of smoke, but like I said, that was much later.

Bheem went out to the scooter and brought two framed photographs wrapped in a khaki paper and a bottle. The pictures were of a group dance number from a movie. In the front row in one and in second row in the other, Shamsie clearly stood out for sheer poise. She lit up when I told her that. Bheem said a shy thank you on both their behalf. 'This is for you. Before returning, we went on a trip to Goa,' he said handing me a bottle of cashew feni.

What did they plan to do with themselves now that they were back?

'Start a dance group for functions like weddings and the like. They call it Orchestra here,' the two replied together. The two 19-year-olds had a cocky air about them, which lifted even my mood.

I stood there, holding the feni bottle, after they had gone. I did not have the heart to tell Shamsie that I had not had a drink in years. That alcohol and I had an all or none relationship. That the bottle of Peter Scot she had gifted me three years ago was still lying somewhere unopened.

My medicine cupboard replenished, I had a deep sleep after three days of restless insomnia. Sometime late at night or early in the morning, I dreamt of Shamsie dancing elegantly in the middle of a vast hall under brightly lit chandeliers. The place looked like a garish movie set like in the pictures Bheem had shown me, but then, it was also a Buddhist monastery with monks in deep meditation sitting in a vast circle, oblivious to the dance. And then, a monk, different from the others, with his round face, narrow eyes, and a three-layered robe, rose majestically, bowed to Shamsie and joined her in dancing. The rhythm became slower, but the movements even more graceful. The chandeliers with their tiny flames swung gently and the monks, deep in their meditation, swayed, chanting in a sing-song manner.

The two danced as a couple in complete harmony with intricate, yet fluid, *abhinaya* movements. As if searching for something, the monk then passed his hands over the pockets of his gown. His dismayed face conveyed he had lost something vital, something on which his very life depended. The dance carried on, the monks kept chanting and the chandeliers still swayed, but the mood was sombre now. After a graceful pirouette, Shamsie opened her palm with a flourish, showing an intricate bronze figure of a dancing girl. She asked with an inquisitive expression, still dancing, but slower, if this was what the monk had lost. The monk, who now looked like Dr Mustafa, with a shimmering cross hanging from his wrist and reading glasses around his neck, shook his head. Through complicated dance gestures, which lasted for a whole minute, the monk conveyed that he had travelled half a continent and still had thousands of 'kos' of travel left. But he had lost his compass. This place is just a stop, and without his compass, he was lost forever—he said with his delicate hand gestures.

In a languid movement, Shamsie opened her palm to show, this time, a tiny compass. Blue and luminescent, the compass was picked up with a smile and a bow by the monk. The two carried on the dance, quicker on their feet, with the other monks swinging merrily to the beat of a slow 'kala doria', which, as Shamsie had told me, Bheem used to sing as a child. The vast praying hall of the monastery was now roofless and the sky a luminous blue compass stretching to the edges of the horizon in all directions.

Nine

Jeet and I stood outside the massive gate of the police station that served hundred odd villages on the north bank of the river, from the school to the pontoon bridge. We had travelled the three kilometers on his bicycle, me sitting on the carrier, because he refused my offer to pedal. He wanted to show off that not only could he manage the cycle with one hand, which I already knew he could, but that he could do it with my weight as well. I told him I had seen him, every morning, carry two large barrels of milk straddled across the cycle, which probably were heavier than me and he did not have to show off, but he insisted. To ride a cycle, he explained, one hand is more than enough. He had got the bell and brake shifted to the left side and that was all there was to it.

'Is it not difficult to apply brake with one hand, that one hand being the left?' I asked.

'If you do not have a right hand, your left becomes as good as the right. You are a doctor. You should know,' he chided. 'Why do you need hands for applying brakes in any case? You just need to be as tall as me and use your feet.' And he showed me how to, by scraping the ground with his chappals and stopping. He was clearly enjoying himself. I would have joined in the mirth, but for the very circumstances which had forced me to sit on his bicycle carrier. My car had been stolen sometime during the night. Jeet was the one who had broken the news, when he came to deliver milk the next morning. 'Your car is gone,' he had said, in a matter of fact manner. And then, with a worried look, he informed me that the Boys stole a car before committing a massacre and abandoned it later.'

'We must go to the police, before they come looking for you,' he advised.

I learnt later that at the police stations in the countryside, the oldest policeman who was often also the one least educated, would be posted as the guard at the entrance. In this case, the entrance was the tall wooden door with metal spikes that reached all the way up to the ceiling and had a trap door cut into it. The main door opened only for jeeps. The 100-year-old mansion, most of it aground, had been inherited a decade back by a doctor working in a far-flung village of Tasmania in Australia. The good doctor had no inkling that the 'haveli' that he now owned and had last seen 10 years back when he had come to India for his father's funeral, had been unofficially appropriated for the internal security of his motherland. This nugget of information was shared by the old policeman when we were on friendlier terms with him, several visits and an equal number of 50-rupee notes later. A cable connected to the electric pole went directly into the ventilator of a room bypassing the metre, and thus, doing away with the irksome responsibility of paying electricity bills.

The old guard, swirling a generous swelling of tobacco from one cheek to the other, listened to us and admonished us sternly. Could we not see in our selfish pursuit that it was far too early in the day? The staff had slept late, because they had returned from surveying the area late last night. Then he asked, 'Why did you not park the car inside the house?'

'I did. It was very much inside the house.'

'Then why did you not put a chain and a lock on the gate?'

'I did. They picked the lock.'

'Was it a brass lock?'

'Yes. Very much so. Definitely a brass lock.'

'A heavy lock?'

'Yes, rather heavy.'

'How heavy?'

'Three hundred grams may be.'

'Was it an Aligarh lock?'

'Yes, I think so.'

'Did you have to just press the lock or also to rotate the key to lock it?'

'No, not just press. Key had to be rotated.'

'Once or twice?'

'Twice.'

Regardless of whether he was impressed or not, I certainly was. If this was a preliminary enquiry by a guard posted outside the station, they were bound to be very thorough inside.

The old guard, after having contemplated all my answers, stroked his beard, and decided that the car was stolen because of our carelessness. He declared that we did not deserve to go inside, at least not just then. 'Come at 11. We will see then.' Jeet put his hand into his pocket, a movement keenly tracked by the wizened eyes. When the 50-rupee note was safe in his own pocket, the guard pushed the trap door a bit to shout deep inside the building, 'It is the *tunda dodhi* and the Bania *daactor* (the one-armed milkman and the Hindu doctor). It seems, a car is stolen.'

I came to know later that the beat policemen sometimes referred to all Hindus as Banias, a term not exactly correct, since Bania was just one of the Hindu castes. But I was flattered they knew us, although Jeet was clearly unhappy at the description about him. When I asked him how they could have known about us, he was both complimentary and caustic, 'They are the police. They know everything. On the other hand, I have heard that it is them who steal cars and lease them out to the Boys.'

'You done with them?' a voiced bellowed from the inside.

'Yes.'

'Bring them in then.'

We walked behind the guard. A tuft of white hair peeked out from under his turban.

'How old are you,' I asked the back of his head.

'Seventy-three. Got this job after my son was killed by the Boys last year, at the Baisakhi massacre. Sahib said age does not matter since all I have to do is stand at the door. Compassionate grounds.'

I was touched. As I put my hand in my pocket to retrieve more money, Jeet stopped me. 'He is lying. I have been seeing him here for 10 years. They just forgot to retire him,' he whispered. I thought Jeet may have been still cut up over the guard's description of him.

The scene inside was that of a medieval public bath. There was a large spread out oval courtyard, surrounded by rooms in various stages of ruin. In the middle was a hand pump. The handle had been taken off and was lying uselessly next to it. An electric motor chugged loudly instead, and a generous stream of water filled the brick-lined water tank. Knee deep inside it, stood the police inspector in charge of the station, in his striped underwear, his sub-inspector, the munshi, the head constable, and three other constables. Their clothing and fire-arms lay on the ground, a safe distance away, to keep the uniforms, the pistols, and the rifles from getting wet.

The inspector's long hair was tied up in a bun on top of his head and his open beard came down to his navel. Hands on his hips, he shouted at the both of us, 'What brings you here?'

I told him about the car in a voice loud enough to carry above the din of the motor. 'We do not have time for petty crimes. The Boys can attack any time. We have to be battle-ready 24x7.'

I looked at the pistols, the rifles, cartridge belts, and uniforms lying far away and nodded dumbly.

'But why did you not park the car inside?'

'I did.'

It seemed that the set of questions inside and outside the police station were standard. I answered each one all over again; details about the weight of the lock, its Aligarh brand, whether I had rotated the key, and how many times.

'People are so careless, and we get disturbed so early in the morning.'

It took some effort not to look at my watch to confirm if it was past 10.

'Where is the *kaapy* of the car?'

'Kaapy', of course, meant the registration booklet.

'In the car,' I thought that should have been obvious.

'Stupid.'

'Aren't we supposed to keep it in the car all the time?'

'Normally yes, but who told you these are normal times? Sometimes, when we reach the car, it is all burnt down in a bomb hit. The only way to know if it is your car is from the chassis number. And that is written only in the *kaapy*.'

'But why would terrorists bomb the car they are travelling in?'

'They wouldn't, but we would. Understood?'

I said I did.

He seemed to suddenly remember something. 'You are a doctor, no?' I said I was.

'You know how to check blood pressure?'

I said yes, I did.

'Sure?'

I said I was sure.

The inspector was out of the tank in a moment and nodded at me to follow him. He was still in his long-striped underwear, which dripped all the way to his office. I guessed his turban, uniform, and revolver were to be brought by a minion. The munshi, who was the station clerk, also in a long, dripping, and striped underwear led Jeet into another office room. To file the report, I presumed.

The inspector's office was a large room and appeared to have been recently hit by an earthquake. Loose bricks from the floor, ceiling, and walls lay scattered. These were 'lakhori' bricks from olden times, flat, thin, and red. Some bricks had been put to use as paperweights for the many files lying about. A table, which from its size seemed to have been a proper eight-seater dining table at some grander point in time, occupied most of the room. There was just one chair. A low ceiling fan that had a black Bakelite switch and no speed regulator came to life like a whirlwind. Some papers that had not been weighed down by the bricks flew off the table and clung to the walls like long lost relatives.

The inspector disappeared under the table to rummage around and I was left looking at his striped behind. He pulled himself out shortly, now holding a blood pressure apparatus and a stethoscope. Both were in surprisingly good condition, considering the rest of the room.

'I busted a terrorist last week. He is still with us. We raided his house and found this on him.

'On him?' I asked looking at the benign device.

'It could have been anything. A newfangled transmitter or a bomb,' he answered as if trying to explain something obvious to a child.

I said, yes, of course, one could not be too careful.

'Check my pressure,' he ordered, sitting in the high-backed chair with his wet right arm straight on the table. I managed to stretch the cuff around the massive arm.

The blood pressure was normal. He wanted it to be done again. Still normal. He looked cheated.

I was curious about the source of the medical gadget.

'Why would a terrorist in his 20s keep a blood pressure apparatus in his house?'

'Who? Oh him. Twenties? He is 55 if a day.'

'Can I check his pressure? He may be a patient if he kept this at home. He may collapse here, and it will be on you.' My empathy for the unknown prisoner was less as a doctor for a patient and more as one patient of blood pressure for another.

The inspector certainly did not want him dying on him, not yet at least. A constable was instructed to carry the apparatus and escort me to the cells. As I passed by the next office, I saw Jeet answering questions about the number plate of my car, its make and model. I sensed there was a negotiation of sorts going on.

The constable unlocked the cell door and, after shoving me inside, locked it from outside.

The Sikh man, to whom the apparatus belonged, had his handcuff chained to a rusted ring in the wall. He had a handsome angular face with a few pockmarks on the forehead and was wearing just a vest and an underwear stained with dark blood which had dried. The open salt and pepper hair and beard were matted with crusts of mud. His arms and legs were covered in bruises, purple, red, and blue in color, like the colors in a puddle of petrol. There were cuts and lacerations of varying shapes and in various stages of healing. Many fresh ones, likely inflicted the night before, were also visible. Despite the circumstances, there was a formality in his bearing.

Maybe this was what had kept the constabulary up until late. He nodded to me stiffly. On seeing the blood pressure apparatus, he relaxed and offered his right arm. I managed to find just enough normal skin to wrap the cuff around. The readings were extremely high. That would happen when a patient goes off medicine abruptly and, instead, gets the treatment that he was getting.

'Where are your medicines?' I wanted to know.

'At home. You think the police would have been kind enough to let me bring my medicines when they pulled me out in the dead of night. Is it very high?'

I told him it was. 'I thought all the holy fighters were youngsters.'

'They are. The police got the wrong guy. Similar name. I am just a history teacher in a school in a village along the river.'

'Did you tell them that?'

'At least a hundred times. I told them I could show them my master's degree in history and pay slips if they would take me home just once. Every time I got slapped with the belt.' He gestured at his bluish red calves, swollen up nearly to the size of his thighs. It made his legs look like pillars.

When Jeet rushed up the stairs that morning, I had just then picked up the strip of tablets for my morning dose. On being told about the stolen car, I had shoved it into my pocket to scramble down the stairs. I pulled it out of my pocket now and let it drop near him. There was a clanking sound of the door being unlocked. As I turned to go, I heard a whispered 'Thank you.'

I was called into the munshi's office by Jeet, where there was an argument going on. On a loose sheet of paper, the munshi had scribbled in Punjabi the number, colour, make, and model of my car and the date, time, and place where I had last seen it.

I was also admonished for driving a car for so many years in P-3 which was not registered here, but in Chandigarh.

'You have been using P-3 roads and paying road tax to some other government.'

I said Chandigarh was the capital of P-3.

'But it is outside P-3. Under another government. We do not get the taxes you pay them,' he said. He was right.

'The state transport authorities have to be informed. Even before the car is found, they will levy a tax, interest and penalty, a total of about five thousand rupees.'

This sum was one fourth of the value of the car.

'Even before?' I thought I had misheard.

'Even before and even if it is not found. Because you have admitted in writing that you have been driving the car here till last night, after you shifted your residence here. That is how it was stolen from here. It could not have been stolen from here if you were driving it in Chandigarh. No?'

I said it did make sense.

But if the munshi was paid five hundred rupees right then, he would forget to tell the transport department. 'Tell me doctor sahib, honestly, with hand on your heart, have you ever heard of a cheaper bargain?'

I was hungry. Just so I could go home and eat my breakfast, I passed the money to him. The only time I actually paid money to check the blood pressure of two patients.

***

The next day I asked Jeet to take me to the second-hand scooter market across the river. He knew a dealer whose expertise lay in assessing whether a scooter was stolen or not. I was wiser after my day at the police station and did not want to buy an old scooter which had been stolen. In the evening, we drove to the police station on the newly bought old scooter cleared by the dealer as not stolen, to check the status of the investigation. We chose to go in the evening to avoid disturbing the staff during their bath. The old guard put up a show of not letting us in. He got another fifty rupees.

'It is not the money. It is the principle,' he insisted.

The munshi sat on his haunches in a vest and the same striped garment, in a far corner of the courtyard, pumping a Primus stove. A freshly carved chicken in a battered aluminum basin lay next to him. The feathers and the rest of the bird were scattered all around.

When we got his attention, I stated the reason of our visit.

'With dozens of people being killed on the streets every day, the police are a bit busy you see,' he said continuing to pump the stove. Kerosene spurted out of the tiny hole at the top and the air became heavy with its smell. 'Kindly bear with us, sir, if we, involved in our mundane preoccupations, have not been able to locate your precious vehicle quickly enough.'

He stood up tall and reed thin in his vest and underwear. His hair and beard open, face twisted in sarcasm, he surveyed the courtyard as if looking for something. There was nothing there, except the chicken feathers sweeping along the floor in the breeze.

'We will get back to you if something comes up,' he said officiously. 'And if you do not leave right now, I will arrest you for disturbing the decorum of the police station.'

He stood tall, facing us in undergarments and saluting somebody behind us. It was the senior inspector who had come out of the loo across the courtyard, his fly still in the process of being buttoned up.

'There you are, Doctor. I was remembering you.' He took me by the elbow and led me to his office. Once again, he disappeared under the table and came out, with the blood pressure apparatus. 'Check it now. It has to be high.'

I did and told him it still was not. He looked like a child who had been robbed of a toy.

'You came for your car, I presume? He retrieved the sheet of paper on which the munshi had jotted down notes the day before and went through a door that cautioned 'Wireless Room. No entry'. The door slammed shut behind him. But he reappeared rather quickly, with a satisfied look on his face.

'Here. Done. I have flashed the message. Every policeman from here up to Ladakh is looking out for your Fiat now.'

'Why Ladakh?' I wondered.

'Because, after that, it is Pakistan on one side, and China on the other, Doctor sahib. My writ does not run in those countries.'

I met Jeet in the corridor who had a hangdog look. 'The munshi says the inspector wants another thousand rupees to write a pucca report.'

I told him not to bother. 'The inspector has already flashed a message in front of me and every cop from here to Ladakh is looking out for my car.'

'In front of you?'

'Not exactly. I could not be taken inside the wireless room. Protocol you know. It is "out of bounds" for civilians,' I told him.

It was dark by the time we came out. I drove to Jeet's village to drop him. There was a police *naka*, a roadblock, outside his village. A stout branch of a tree probably from the storm last week was used to block the road. Two policemen, in a makeshift wooden hut, lay deep asleep in plastic chairs. An empty pint of Bagpiper and a crumpled packet of Bikaneri munchies lay discarded on the floor.

Jeet chuckled, 'All cops right up to Ladakh are looking for your car, Doctor sahib? That is what you said, no?'

'I will go tomorrow and give him his thousand rupees,' he added.

Ten

The next afternoon, I was examining the only patient who had come till then. A retired army man, with legs swollen like pillars and testicles like cricket balls, who had spent many years in Orissa.

'Filaria,' I told him. As I looked for my prescription pad, the door burst open, a hurricane of khaki came in and several guns were pointing at me all in a fraction of a second. The ex-subedar slunk away real fast, despite his elephantiasis. I was carried by four policemen, one attached to each limb, my stethoscope dangling from my neck, and heaved on to the back of a Gypsy like a dead calf.

The jeep hurtled on the pot-filled road and my back hurt wherever it touched the bumping metal of its floor. I tried to sit up and was pushed back by the heel of a boot. Four commandos, their faces covered with black scarves, sat on the sides. I could see the clouds waft against the sky and the overhanging trees rush past. My brain worked fast like that of a trapped animal. It had been, I guessed, 20 minutes at that speed, and we had not taken any turn. So, we were past the Gayab Road and I was not being taken to the Gym.

I relaxed a little. After another five minutes, the jeep took a left turn and slowed down a lot. Then it was bobbing up and down like a boat. The pontoon bridge, of course! We were crossing the river. I knew there was a hulk of a ruin on the city side, which served as a large police station. A head quarter of sorts, in fact.

The ground floor of the police station was flooded with muddy water. I was shoved up a narrow flight of stairs, although I could have walked up on my own perfectly well. After a short walk, I was pushed into a cell along a corridor, the end of which I could not see, because it was dark in there. Dark and damp. Like a cave, with many swarthy policemen waddling with their bludgeons as cave men. I asked my escort why the police station was built in water. That was all I could think of. Was it a security thing? He looked at me with amusement. He must have found it odd that I was concerned about the location of the police station, given the circumstances. 'We are the ones who ask questions here,' he barked, and a clunky bolt was pushed home. The loud metallic sound echoed back and hung in the air. The policeman came back though, 'Since you ask, it is the river which changed course. The police have not moved for a hundred years since this was built. And will not. Rivers come and go.'

I sat there on the cold floor of the unevenly plastered cement that oozed water. An hour later I was taken to a bigger room and made to sit on a wooden stool, my feet barely reaching the floor. This was a tall stool like the one in my childhood home. My father used it to change the light bulbs and to remove the blades of the ceiling fans when summer ended. He would then wrap those in old clothes and store them away.

There was a table with ink stains like the one in the village school I went to. A wood and cane low chair was placed on the other side of the table. It seemed the chair had been carved out of a three-seater couch, because it had no arms. A plump man, whose paunch flowed over his belt, held me down to the stool as if I were going to get up and make a bolt for it. He smelt of garlic and that reminded me, I had not had lunch. When I asked him if they were sure they did not have the wrong man, he answered, 'You are the doctor, aren't you?'

'I am one but there are other doctors, you know.'

'Tell it to Maai-baap. He is coming from the Gurukul just to talk to you, on a Sunday morning, leaving his golf halfway. Our orders were just to lift you up and deliver you here.' He sounded crisply professional. As if he worked for a courier company and I was a parcel waiting to be handed over to the consignee.

In Hindi, *maai* is mother and *baap*, father. Sometimes, senior officers are called that, as a gesture of supplication before a powerful yet benevolent authority. A parental Yin and Yang.

'I am obliged that he is taking out time for me,' I said. I was, too, because otherwise I would have been in the cell for another day at least. Not that there was any guarantee even now that I would not be in the cell for another day or a month or a year or more.

Maai-baap turned out to be a short and overweight sardarji with curled moustache and a glistening black beard tied tightly in a fine black net, the upper ends of which disappeared under a golf cap. He was dressed for golf in a t-shirt, trousers, and sneakers.

'Are you or are you not the doctor?' He seemed impatient to get back to the Gurukul.

'I am a doctor. There are others, sir. Maybe you got the wrong...'

'You think we are assholes!' said he, except in Punjabi, which sounded even worse. He pounded the table for a quick answer from me.

I said no, I did not think that at all, but maybe his subordinates had got the wrong doctor. They were busy, and it was human to make mistakes.

I was sure that it was not his own office we were in. He wanted to get back to his blessed game as soon as he could, and he had me brought to the nearest police station. The chair was too low for him and my stool and the table too high. This did not augur well for me at all. 'So, you are a smart aleck. I could send you to the Gym, where bodies go in but only information comes out. Imagine a cane crusher, and you would get a rough idea. I am interested only in the juice. That would also save me time.'

My mind was all about the inferiority complex this mismatch of furniture spelt for Maai-baap and for me. He was a short man sitting in a low chair, who routinely faced taller suspects sitting on a higher stool on the other side.

Just how many poor sods had Maai-baap sent to the Gym
to compensate? Perhaps I had lost my mind, because at a
time when I should have been wetting my pants, my mind
was coming up with furniture commercials instead. 'Ikea
Office Furniture: Saving Poor Sods for 75 Years. Ting, tong.'

I reminded myself of the cane crusher to focus, 'But you
have not asked me anything yet. Please do ask, sir.'

'Where is your *bluddy kaar*?'

'It was stolen. From my house on the river. At night,
three days ago,' I wondered how my car had turned from an
object of total apathy to a subject of this intense investigation,
making senior police officers interrupt their golf to look for it.

'Fine. I thought you might say this. Let us suppose it was
stolen. Just for the sake of argument. How come you did not
report it then?'

He had a 'gotcha' look and probably a smile under his
moustache. I told him I did. I did report.

'How come it does not figure in the list of crimes
reported within the police jurisdiction of your home then?
The last stolen car in that area was reported four years ago,
and it was a police car.'

I told him about the bribe I had given and the bribe I had
not. That the report of the stolen car was still kutcha on a loose
paper, which lay in the inspector's top right drawer, pending
full payment. I thought he sensed right away a ring of truth in
my account of the paid and the balance bribe money.

He scowled, caught the edge of the table, and heaved
himself out of the chair. He turned around and walked to

a room behind his chair, separated just by a green curtain. I heard some orders being given over the phone which mentioned my name, a sheet of loose paper, and a table drawer. There was a long pause, another brief conversation and Maai-baap was back minus the scowl.

'You can go now.'

It was as if he had difficulty uttering those words. As if he had hardly let off anybody else before.

'Has my car been found, sir?'

'Hmm. Let us say it has been sighted. We will find it.'

I did not expect what came next.

'Have you heard of Ghalib?' Maai-baap looked happy now that he was going straight back to golf, but I failed to get the Ghalib connection.

I nodded my head to say I had and tried to remember if I had missed my medication. I had not.

'*Zaahid sharaab peene de masjid mein baith kar,*
Ya wo jagah bata de jahan par khuda na ho.'

(O Priest, allow me to sit and drink inside the mosque or tell me of a place where there is no God.)

He recited it three times just for emphasis. I stared dumbly at him. He provided the context.

'Police is like "khuda", you see. We are everywhere.'

I must still not have looked enlightened. So he changed the topic.

'But if and when we do find your car, you are unlikely to get it back anytime soon. If it has been used in a crime, there would be formalities of the long-drawn type.'

I should have said that I understood or something to that effect, but what came out of the mouth of fussy me was, 'That is not by Ghalib.'

The head constable standing next to his chair hit my hand lying on the table so hard with his stick, I almost fainted. Through the haze, I heard him say, '*Maai-baap naal jabaan larhanda hain, daactor? Ghar jaana ki nahin? Bol Gaalab* (Doctor, not argue with Maai-baap. Do you want to go home or not? Say Gaalab)!'

I said, 'Gaalab.'

The golf cap bobbed up and then down, accepting my apology of sorts. I was told I could go home now.

'But do not leave the town without permission,' Maai-baap added sternly.

'I do not live in a town,' I tried to explain.

'Or the village or whatever,' he said as if it was self-explanatory.

I did not want to be found in infringement of any official order and clarified that the 'whatever' was a standalone house on the riverbank.

'Okay, okay. Then do not leave that house,' he was exasperated and in a hurry to get back.

'I have to buy groceries.'

'Do you want me to throw you back in the cell?'

I said no. I came down the stairs and sloshed through the ankle-deep water on the ground floor. My shoes made squelching sounds as I walked out into the sunlight. I cradled my injured right hand in the left one and found Jeet standing next to my new old scooter across the road. He quietly motioned for me to sit on the pillion and drove home without saying a word. I found his behaviour strange, but after what had just happened, perhaps nothing was strange. I realized that he made up for his absent right hand while driving by keeping the scooter at a slow speed and maneuvering it in a zigzag manner, much like he drove his bicycle.

At home, he made us tea and found some biscuits.

He then told me that five Boys, armed with AK-47s, had attacked the police station in the morning and shot the inspector, the munshi, the head constable, and the three constables, while they were having their bath. The water in the tank was thick with blood according to villagers who had ventured into the station later. Before leaving, the Boys had taken with them the middle-aged history teacher whose blood pressure I had checked and to whom I had given my own medicines.

The old watchman was alive, as he had gone to the other side of the road to urinate and had hid in the fields. But he had noted down the description and the number of the car. It was my car. Suddenly, the day, ghastly as it had been, did not seem bizarre at all. Things made sense, and I was not crazy.

Jeet said that the history teacher, in addition to his teaching credentials, was also reputed to be the dreaded mastermind and ideologue of the Liberation Army, known to everybody as General Dhillon. Even I had heard of him.

The irony of the couplet recited by Maai-baap dawned on me. It could also mean, let us unleash a massacre right inside a police station, since the police are present everywhere anyway. The saviours of General Dhillon must also have not just read the couplet, but also interpreted it the same way. But all I could think of at that moment was that I hoped they knew it was not 'Gaalab' who wrote it. I was not a big fan of Urdu poetry, but my dad, when he was feeling kindly towards me one evening after his drink, had chosen to impart this information. The context was my religious mother's admonition, who had a nook in the house with divine pictures which she called her temple. 'If you have to drink, drink outside the house.'

He had recited the couplet to me when my mother was in the other room.

'Most people think this is by Ghalib, except it is not.'

After a while, 'You won't ask who wrote it?'

I was nine. 'Who?'

'Not known. Anonymous. Could have been written by me to tell your mother.'

Eleven

Shamsie was now known to everyone except Bheem and Sidhu, as Jassi. She did not like the name, but Sidhu had insisted on it, after a Punjabi movie set in Europe became a rage. The lead character in that movie was a dancer named Jassi.

Shamsie tied a clothesline across the small backyard and spread Bheem's and her clothes on it. These she would iron later for the show tonight. The landlady, her face taut with anger, sprang out of her room.

'I thought we had the last word on it. That you will not spread your undergarments here for my husband to ogle at.'

'The last word was that the backyard is for us and the front courtyard for you. If your husband has a sick mind, you should change him.'

'At least, I have a husband unlike some women I know,' the landlady retorted, her face still indignant.

'Well, I have Bheem. What is it that he does not do that your husband does?' Jassi asked over the washing line, her hair tied in a bun. 'Except eyeing other women's bras?'

The landlady, plump from her sedentary work tending to the grocery store out of her house, asked Shamsie yet once again, 'You are shameless. Why did you not tell us you two were not married when you came to rent the room?'

'You did not ask,' Shamsie reminded the older woman like before.

They lived in one room in the three-cubicle brick house in a honeycomb-like colony of thousands of such tenements. The colony was called Dhakka Colony. In Punjabi, the word 'dhakka' meant force and the name unhesitatingly implied it was a colony of squatters. The squatters were eligible voters of varied castes, a vote-bank which generations of politicians had banked upon during election time. In return for their votes, they could live on what was government land, originally meant for a sports stadium according to the master plan of the city. When one bought a 500 square feet of house here, one did not get any title or a piece of paper from the previous owner, one was given just the key to the house. Elected leaders, with their eye on the next election cycle, not only helped perpetuate the occupation over decades, but had thoughtfully provided electricity, water, and sewage connections. These services were free of charge since these houses did not exist on paper. Bills could not be sent to non-existent houses. But the services did not always work, because even without Dhakka Colony, they stretched too thin across rest of the city. In addition, no budget could be allotted for the maintenance of a ghost colony which did not exist in any government file even if it were right there in your face sprawling across hundreds of acres with its lanes, bye-lanes and overflowing sewers.

Dhakka Colony was often touted to be the fourth largest off-the-record colony in the country. This meant that somebody had gone to the extent of recording the population of all such unrecorded, ghost colonies. Which was unlikely, but there it was, large enough. The hundred and fifty thousand odd adult inhabitants of Dhakka Colony were officially registered as voters at their permanent addresses in their ancestral villages spread all over the state. That is where they went to vote each election season. To vote was the squatters' code of honor. That was the least they could do. The understanding was that as long as they voted and voted en-bloc, they got to keep the houses, whichever party won. The polling percentage of voters from Dhakka Colony in the last elections was 94.5 per cent, as compared to the national average of 56.5 per cent.

As the evening sun went down, swarms of young men dressed in white shirts, dark trousers, and black ties emerged from nooks and crannies of Dhakka Colony and went into the city either walking or in autorickshaws cramped eight to one. These were the waiters of the city. The ones who waited upon clients in restaurants, clubs, and hotels all over the sprawling metropolis. An hour later, young girls in fetching dresses inspired by popular Bollywood dance numbers would hail autorickshaws and disappear into the city night, some of them accompanied by stocky male escorts. These were the dancing girls who performed at weddings, ring ceremonies, anniversaries, and birthday parties till late into the night. The girls who were to head to nearby villages travelled by cabs or canters, which were utility vans fitted with seats. To save money, they often shared vehicles with men of the wedding band going to the same wedding. The band men wore shiny red dresses with turbans and epaulettes and high shoes. Their brass trumpets, trombones, and drums took up more space than the men themselves. The band and the dancers would go to the same wedding, but they performed different jobs and at different times. The band led the wedding party to the bride's house earlier in the evening. The girls would dance later when the guests were roaring drunk.

When it was pitch dark, another bunch of girls with risqué dresses and heavy makeup would step out. They waited for drivers of swanky cars to pick them up one by one, but sometimes in small groups too. Those who did not get picked up, walked into the city on their own. The dancers considered themselves artists and shunned the hookers.

By daybreak, all of them would be back—the waiters, the dancers, and the hookers, except the dancing troupes and the band men who had gone outstation. They would be back just in time to see the freshly washed factory workers queueing up at the bus stop and the bleary-eyed middle-aged women, in their grubby salwar-kameezes, who would cross the wide road and slip into the city to clean, cook, and launder for people with proper houses. They would be followed sometime later by their husbands dressed in faded dungarees, the municipal sweepers' uniform. The husbands would sweep the streets, collect garbage, and go down the sewers to ensure free flow.

Dhakka Colony thus provided grist to the urban mill 24 hours a day, seven days a week. Over the years, the city and the colony had come to develop a stout symbiotic relationship and it was not possible to imagine one without the other. Some years back, a PhD scholar from the city university conducted a survey supported by a grant from an American foundation. It found that 95 per cent of people in the colony were Dalits, while the city had exactly the reverse caste ratio. The survey went on to argue that this exploitative arrangement perpetuated the centuries-old Manuvadi tradition of confining Dalits to certain jobs and certain spaces.

At a barber shop in the colony, a bald old man, who came there just to read the newspaper, spat into the drain in front of the shop, and said to the waiting clients, 'Idiots. They could have asked me about the percentages. Why waste money on a survey?'

The said scholar left the city after she found, to her horror, a heap of stinking garbage blocking her driveway one fine morning. It was suspected that the sweepers from Dhakka Colony had done it. Stuck in it was a message that read, 'You do not understand. So, shut up.'

A week later, the city office of the American research foundation was ordered shut by the city authorities for committing acts prejudicial to the social and cultural harmony of India.

Beyond Dhakka Colony was a four-lane road called 'Bypass Road', with the New Bus Terminus across from it. This was the edge of city. The bypass was constructed three years back, so that long distance traffic did not have to pass through the city, thus saving time and decreasing congestion on the city roads. The main bus station was shifted from the city centre to the new site and was called the new bus station to distinguish it from the old bus station. It was all planned and futuristic. Within three years, the city had grown like a cancer far beyond the bypass. The new bus station was now the default city centre. Haphazard buildings as far the eye could see, and a couple of smoke belching factories completed the picture. The urban planners in the city secretariat were already in parleys to construct a new bypass to bypass the bypass. And a newer bus station to replace the new bus station.

Outside the bus station on the highway, stood a six storied building with hundreds of nine by nine cubicles. These served as offices for travel agents, sex specialists and quacks, the last of whom promised harried wives a cure for their husbands' alcoholism ('Trust me sister, he will puke if he even sees a picture of a bottle'). There were also agents of fairness creams and coaching centres for English, each of which claimed to have been approved by the British Council, (although British Council was unlikely to have known they existed) and assured an IELTS score of 5.5 or above, the minimum required to go abroad as cooks and maids. In addition, there were offices of orchestras, dancing groups, and wedding bands. And, lastly, there were offices promising easy loans as well as those promising easy recovery of loans.

The front elevation of the building was a massive cement wall pockmarked with hundreds of holes, which were the office windows. An architectural monstrosity in its own right, it was further splattered with signboards of various shapes and colours, like postal stamps on an overweight long-distance envelope. The sex specialists' boards had pictures of muscular men with bushy moustaches, the travel agents had aeroplanes and fairness cream companies had pale film heroines. Standing on the road, if you could crane your neck up to the fourth floor, one of the sign boards showed a dancing girl with a passable resemblance to Jassi.

Sidhu pulled the two fruit carts blocking the entrance apart to go into the building. The erratic lift had crashed a few times and regulars left it alone. He ambled across to the stairs and, taking two steps at a time reached the fourth floor. He unlocked the door with the dancing Jassi poster. Sidhu had simply taken a Pakeezah poster and replaced Meena Kumari's head with Jassi's. It looked seamless at first sight. He was a graduate from the distance education department of a university that was later shut down for producing more graduates than the adult population of the state. It was suspected they sold fake degrees to whoever paid. Not that Sidhu required a formal degree. His father owned large tracts of land and he did not need a job. Besides, he was a wizard with musical instruments. Coming from generations of religious singers, he played harmonium, tabla, sitar, guitar, drums, and harmonica like a natural. Sidhu took off from work from November to February, when there were no weddings because of the inauspicious arrangement of stars, to take his parents to Anandpur Sahib, Paonta Sahib, and the distant Hazur Sahib and Patna, the pilgrimage circuit for the Sikhs. Once in two or three years, during summers, he also took them to Hemkunt Sahib, which was snowbound in winters. The rest of the year, he worked all seven days, and nights too, when there were performances. Sometimes, his father and he would be the accompanists when a performance included Jassi's solo dance at sober day-time functions.

Sidhu was a baptized Sikh. He would be in the office at 8 in the morning, after offering prayers at the gurudwara on his way, and for eight hours he would be alone on that floor in the giant shell of a building. The fourth floor was the least preferred by tenants, since the lift was not safe, and hence the rent was less than the other floors. As a symbol of his baptized status, Sidhu wore a kirpan over his white kurta. He could get a much better job in one of the music companies in Civil Lines and work in air-conditioned studios with fancy equipment if he wanted. But, he adored Shamsie and admired Bheem.

There was a rather long, but interesting story behind Sidhu's baptism. It was involuntary when it happened, even though now not only did he accept it, but also followed all the commandments to the letter, including the ones about abstaining from alcohol. He was even proud of his special status. He chose to wear the kirpan over his kurta, unlike his father who wore it under. His father thought a true Sikh was known by his behaviour and not by the religious accessories he wore. But it had been him who had, with the help of his two brothers and three neighbours, carried his kicking and screaming 25-year-old son to the Golden Temple in Amritsar three years ago. After Sidhu was pushed through the Deori of the Golden Temple, held by his arms on both sides, he was mesmerized by the sheer beauty of the wide-open space. The marble pathways, vast pool of water, and the gold-plated top of the majestic gurudwara calmed him, especially the soft music that suffused the cool morning air. He stopped resisting and went through the rituals of being baptized, starting with a dip in the *sarovar*, willingly and enthusiastically.

The forced visit had been a last-ditch effort by Sidhu's father to treat his rebellious son's drinking. Sidhu's drinking was not much if one went by the amount and frequency. But it was shocking in a family, where nobody over generations had been known to have touched alcohol.

The medical treatments, the few that were resorted to, and faith healers of all denominations in various dresses and robes had failed miserably to find a cure. When the desperate father locked Sidhu up in a room, he disappeared through a window. He was found a month later by the police of the country of Greece, travelling in a decrepit fishing trawler with 20 other Punjabi youth on forged passports. They were on one of the several legs of journey to England that had been organized by a travel agent. When deported, and questioned by the Indian police, Sidhu had replied proudly that travel was in his blood; his great grandfather had travelled from Hongkong to Vancouver by an illegal Japanese ship, Komagata Maru, along with four hundred other Punjabi men who were not allowed to disembark at the destination. The ship, as everybody knew, was forced to return to India after remaining parked off shore for two months, because the authorities refused to let it in. Upon its arrival at Calcutta harbour, British soldiers had shot dead several of those men, to quell a riot, it seems.

When the police asked Sidhu's father if the story about his grandfather was true, that his grandfather had indeed been a part of this fabled journey of freedom fighters, he agreed it was.

'But he did not drink. Did he?' He had shouted at his son when the police were gone.

Sidhu mixed music, his speciality being making Punjabi folk songs even peppier using modern instruments. He had composed for some singers and even copyrighted three albums of his own. The inebriated men who came to attend a celebration were used to film songs that the girls lip-synced and danced to. Sidhu's music and his DJ skills made Jassi's shows different. His music equipment, which was his personal and comprised of a stereophonic player, a synthesizer, and the boom speakers, was the only reason the Jassi troupe office needed to be double locked securely. Apart from Bheem and Jassi, he was the only permanent member of the troupe. Three other girls and four bhangra dancers were hired as and when required, were paid per performance, and changed from one night to the other. The bhangra dancers were required more for their heft than dancing skills. They danced in a ring around the girls to discourage excitable clients from climbing the stage.

Sidhu spent the whole day in office sitting next to the telephone waiting for bookings. Shamsie stayed at home. Bheem drove around villages on his Vespa for marketing 'Jassi Dance Orchestra'. This division of labour was Bheem's choice. Sidhu had offered himself for the outdoor work, which the three of them agreed he could do equally well if not better, since he was more talkative and persuasive of the two. Moreover, he was a Jat, and the most expensive weddings happened in Jat households, other than in some Hindu business families in cities. But the one who managed the office and answered the phone calls was required to deal with fresh inquires and had to be a salesman with sharp negotiating skills. Bheem lacked these qualities altogether. Besides, Bheem loved to drive along the canals that criss-crossed the countryside. Bheem also liked to sing while driving and preferred a travelling job. He liked to not just hum, but sing full throat, as if that were all that mattered in that moment.

His scooter was pasted over with stickers of a cavorting Jassi. He carried a stack of brochures which had pictures from past performances and testimonials from satisfied customers, most of whom would have been happily drunk at the time of writing ('*Balle-balle, fatte chak te Jassi ne*' was the commonest expression of appreciation). Also, there were rate quotes, timings, and conditions (no climbing on the stage, drinks okay but no refilling during a dance, no shouting obscenity, and no celebratory firing in the air). He also carried an appointment diary and a receipt book in case there were spot bookings. Spot bookings were rare. Mostly the clients called back, and Sidhu took over from there.

Bheem was 15 when his mother died. Her feet had slipped on the moss-covered surface when she bent forward to draw water. The well in the Vehra did not have a parapet then. Money was being collected for that and they were still 200 rupees short. He remembered the crowd around the well when the diver went down. Her head had a gash where it had crashed against the wall. She died before even hitting the water, people in the crowd had said.

They cremated her in the far corner of the Vehra, which functioned as the crematorium. For days, water from the well was crimson, the colour getting lighter with each passing day. Until the water became crystal clear, the Vehra women walked one kilometre each day to fetch water from the irrigation channel, which carried canal water to the sarpanch's fields. After the cremation, Bheem did not come home for two days. He wandered along the canals, slept in the fields at night, and blamed himself for his mother's death, for not having volunteered that day to pull water out of the well. He also blamed himself for having caused her pain with his left-handedness during childhood. He was brought home by the Vehra elders, but he did not talk much except later with Shamsie who was, at that time, in the hostel, 50 km away. But she would take a bus every day after school to spend time with Bheem on the canal bridge till late. For long, the two sat on the bridge parapet late into the night, sometimes talking, but mostly quiet.

It took a month for their teenage minds to be able to temper Bheem's self-flagellation. It took even longer for him to go back to the school on the highway, which was now a senior school. The following summer, Comrade Ram too died of skin cancer, which doctors said was because of the tanning chemicals he worked with. Bheem left school and, like all the other boys from the Vehra, started working as a farm labourer, until Shamsie suggested the two go away to Bombay. He had agreed right away, just so he would not have to be alone.

Bheem loved to sing, but he did not sing at any of Shamsie's stage shows. Nobody sang there other than Sidhu's stereo system. Besides, the songs Bheem sang were lilting, but the words were not celebratory. He grew to like driving around villages and meeting new people. The old men playing cards under trees, children playing cricket in the lanes, and the women travelling in tractor trolleys.

But Bheem went to all the orchestra events. The dancing went on till very late and people got rowdier with every passing hour. Shamsie's safety could not be left to Sidhu who was good with gadgets and strong if it came to a fight, but alone, he would not have been enough if there was trouble. Sidhu did not drink but was very touchy when it came to Shamsie and lacked tact. He could, in fact, trigger a fight entirely on his own. Herein, Bheem, having worked as a bouncer in a Bombay dance bar, came in handy.

That morning, Bheem was happy with his work. He had completed nine villages on one side of the canal, and it was not even noon yet. More importantly, he had in his pocket the advance money for two weddings in the coming month. In every village, he would first go to a central place, which almost always was a banyan tree under which men played cards when it was too hot to work. He would tell them about his group and learn from them which families had a wedding fixed in the coming months. Also, the state had at least three major elections in five years, not counting the odd bye-election. During the two months of campaigning, candidates held dance events to entertain voters. Country liquor was on the house and opium a take-home gift.

Bheem would gather bits and pieces of information about his prospective clients from the card players, park his scooter under their charge and go around the village on foot with brochures in a sling bag. The sling bag was gifted to him at a conference of farm workers, where he had sung a few songs. The bag had travelled with him to half the rural hinterland of the state, and since it had a sickle and hammer printed in red, the boys playing *gulli-danda* in the village lanes started calling him Comrade Bheem. Bheem himself cared nothing about politics. All he knew was, he felt exhilarated while singing songs written by Udasi and Lal Singh. The fact that these poets were Dalits was incidental to him. He sang those songs, because they were songs about him and all that he remembered. They were about Shamsie too, but she asked him to sing just to hear his deep voice and the way his face looked when he sang. She would sit just looking at him transfixed till the song finished.

As he drove his scooter that afternoon along the wide canal, he playfully touched every overhanging branch he passed under and sang:

> 'When the labourer woman
> Roasts her heart on the tawa,
> The moon laughs from behind the tree,
> The father amuses the younger one,
> Making music with bowl and plate;
> The older one tinkles the bells
> Tied to his waist,
> And he dances,
> These songs do not die
> nor either the dance...'

Twelve

One March morning, I was jolted awake while it was still dark, by the sound of the hand pump downstairs. The hand pump was inside the gate, which was locked at night, so somebody had scaled the wall. The last thing I wanted at that time was somebody stealing my scooter. I sprang out of the bed sick with worry. During the day, I kept the gate unlocked to let patients know I was home and to let passers-by drink water if they were thirsty. It was a long road, and this was the only hand pump between the school and the pontoon bridge.

On my last visit, Dr Mustafa had asked about the content of my dreams. So, I had let him know about the one I had the night after I met him, in which he looked like Hiuen Tsang who had lost his compass, but still danced divinely. He looked pleased and, from his drawer, gave me a whole two months' supply of a new antidepressant, which had not yet reached the Indian market. The drug worked so well that, for the first time in months, I felt like seeing patients. Jeet said it had to happen, since he had never heard of a doctor retiring. Patients were quick to sense my interest from the light-hearted way I spoke to them. Reema always said that I had a good sense of humour. A bit dry though, she had added.

There had been a steady trickle of patients every day, throughout the month. And a couple of times at night too. But patients would not jump the wall. If the gates were locked, they would press the bell next to the sign board bearing my name. Through a gap in the window curtains, I saw a mini truck parked at the gate. It was a modified version, not exactly legal, fitted with seats at the back, on which sat two men with shiny red turbans and jackets with epaulettes and brass buttons. A large saxophone, trombone, and two drums were secured with nylon ropes to a metal carrier fitted above the driver's cabin. There were peals of laughter from the courtyard, like people frolicking with water. Whoever it was, they were neither terrorists, nor police. None of the two would be keen on frolic or the saxophones.

I wrapped a shawl around myself and came out of my room. The tall girl at the hand pump, decked up in a dark ghagra-choli with shiny spots, was Shamsie. She was washing off her makeup and splashing water at a man, who hid behind the waiting room door to escape getting wet. When she saw me come down the stairs, she squealed—'Daactor Sahib!'

Sprinting across the courtyard with those long legs of hers, she threw her arms around me. My first thought was that I was shorter than her and barely reached her eyebrows. The second was that she carried a strong smell of perfume, vodka, and lime.

'Hey, you are drunk at 4:30 in the morning. Where are you all going?' I asked.

'Let me put that straight right away, Doctor Sahib. We are not going. We are coming back...'

She was more drunk than I had thought. The last time I had seen her slur like this was when she was a schoolgirl, lying in the clinic, recovering from the injection I had given her.

'...from a dance performance of Jassi Orchestra at a village, 10 kilometres up the river. Jassi is yours truly's stage name. Do you know which song I danced on today? Let me show you.'

She slipped off her *kolhapuri*s and did a proper jig for me on the wet grass.

Kala Shah Kala
Mera kala hai sardar.
Gorean nu dafa karo
Mein aap tilley di taar
Gorean nu dafa karo'
(I like my lover dark as he is. Let the fair ones go to hell.)

She had a smooth trained voice, just right for fast Punjabi numbers, and danced with quick and light graceful steps. She took a bow and picked up from where she had left off.

'We were thirsty and thought, well, this is a familiar house. Let me say hello to my charming doctor. And yes, for your kind information, we drink after every performance.

To celebrate. At least, Bheem and I do. Sidhu here is a pucca Sikh, so he is a teetotaller.'

A young man with a white turban and kurta-churidar emerged from the waiting room.

'Meet Mr Sidhu. Our musician, stage manager, and DJ. Do not miss the kirpan he is carrying. That is because he is Amritdhari, and hence, cannot drink, poor fellow.'

I told her that she had already told me that.

'Yes. What I have not told you is that I think he secretly loves me. He is quite a gentleman for a Jat. But then, I have Bheem, no?'

The tall young man in white was clearly wishing he were not there.

'That reminds me, where is my Kala Shah?' Shamsie asked.

'If you shut up for a moment, you might hear him sing,' Sidhu chided her. We could hear Bheem's mellifluous voice from the terrace. On hearing the commotion, he came down and shook hands with me shyly, 'I am sorry we woke you up at this hour. It was entirely Shamsie's idea.'

The group stayed with me until the evening. The three band men (there was another one in the washroom, I found out later) too stayed, although they were casual hires, just sharing the ride. They could not have gone earlier anyway, because after a breakfast of omelettes, which Bheem cooked in my kitchen, Shamsie crashed on my bed and did not wake up for hours. By then, Bheem and one of the men from the band, also a professional cook, had already prepared lunch.

I had never hosted any guests in that house before. Their presence reminded me that I needed to go to the city the next morning for groceries. I was also to see Dr Mustafa and get a fresh supply of the new antidepressant. There was no need to service the car since I no longer had a car. One chore less. I was told that the car had been found charred and the shell was case material in the court's custody. The insurance company needed to examine the shell and take pictures before they could pay me 12,000 rupees, the depreciated value of the car. For getting the court's permission to do so, the court clerk was asking for a thousand rupees. It was not the money, it was the principle, he had said.

During the day, I kept going down to the clinic to examine patients and then coming up to play the host, something I had not done in a very long time.

Before they left, Shamsie took me aside to the terrace for a medical tip. It was getting dark. Her shiny suit looked less incongruous. She said, her problem was stage fright. When she walked to the stage and received the usual welcome with a series of whistles and catcalls, her heart pounded fast. She had to grip the microphone tightly with both hands. The more she became aware of her jitteriness, stronger became the urge to bolt from the stage.

'I never had it in Bombay during auditions or rehearsals. Not even at the dancing school, where people actually knew what dance is.'

'What do you think? Why here then?' I asked.

Her back was towards the sun setting at the far end of the river and her face was in a shadow. Like an infinity pool, the river was flowing into the setting sun, trying to empty itself before the sun vanished.

'Because they are all Jats,' she said, followed by a long pause. 'They are the only ones who can afford such weddings.'

'And you a Chamar? Is that it? I thought you were one kickass Chamar girl.'

Shamsie's face was in the dark and I was not sure if she had tears in her eyes. 'I am. Except when I am onstage, standing under the lights, in front of so many of them. I feel exposed then, like I am not wearing anything. I feel they are jeering at me. I feel, they know.'

She then told me about some banal facts: that there were no toilets in the village, and everyone used the fields instead, but the Vehra people did not own any fields. That the girls walked as far into the Jat fields as they possibly could. That their mothers taught them how to do it cleverly as they grew up. That raping a girl from the Vehra was a coming-of-age ritual for Jat boys. That she had escaped with just her clothes torn and bruises on the thighs, because she got hold of a stone, while lying pinned down.

The sun had sunk into the river and I could see her face better. There were tears alright, but also a jaunty smile.

'He still goes around with an artificial tooth. Was a Jat boy from school, two years ahead of me.'

I took out the packet of cigarettes from my pocket, tore a piece from the cover and wrote the name of a medicine to be taken an hour before performance. It was a beta blocker, used for palpitations and tremulousness, but many performers also used it for stage fright, since it had no sedative effect. I had used it myself, when presenting seminars during my first year in England, when I was self-conscious in the new country to the point of being paranoid.

'Remember, Bheem does not know. Nobody does.'

I nodded.

Before going down, she hugged me like in the morning, when she had been drunk and exuberant. It was an awkward, but warm, feeling. I had not been hugged in decades. I thought I had not missed it.

I was not even the hugging type. My mother once told Reema in my defence, 'It is not his fault. Even as a small child, he would cuddle stiffly.'

I slept early to make up for my lost sleep. I dreamt of the river being awash with dead bodies that tumbled fast over one another in the flow, as if competing in a race. In the haste, they would get entangled with each other. Arms of one with the legs of another, slowing down till the flow of water separated them impatiently, as if they were two fighting kids. Then they would again join the marathon of the dead, going faster and faster to make up for the lost time. Some of them were freshly dead with red spots in the centre of their forehead, like people coming out of a Hanuman temple on a Tuesday evening.

'PMI, sweetheart, is one to two hours,' would say tall and skinny Enid. PMI meant 'post-mortem interval' or simply the time between death and the autopsy. Recently divorced Enid was the Welsh forensic pathologist whom I used to assist, at autopsies, during my locum jobs in Bristol. Since she could be called anytime of the day or night, she often smelled of scotch, perfume, and mint. But her 'Sweetheart PMIs', as these came to be known, were never wrong. Even the judges knew that. In the river of my dream, many of the dead had PMIs of an hour or two. They were the nimble ones, gliding past each other like ballerinas.

'This is a stiff one, luv. Arms akimbo. You cannot force them in. Looks like a scarecrow, doesn't he? With that hole in the head, I bet you fifty pounds he fell dead just like that. Like Jesus on the cross. He was not moved for two hours at least. PMI, sweetheart, 20 hours in the Bristol weather of last night. But here, in this smouldering hell of yours, it may be just six,' I heard her say in my dream.

There were many more, the likes of which I had never seen before. There were some green and bloated, bobbing up and down on the waves. So, I asked Enid, who was looking fresh and bright with jasmine flowers strung in her hair and not drunk at all.

'These have been dead for a while. PMI, sweetheart, is two or three days. They forgot to throw them in the river for a while, it seems. Your guys here are getting lazy.'

She had now walked up to me and the jasmine fragrance was making me dizzy. Together we saw shrivelled black ones now, gliding along the water, shooting like arrows and running past the laggard greens.

'My, my!' Her professional curiosity aroused, she turned around to ask, 'Where did they get them from? Egypt? These mummies are from some earlier revolution, not this one. Tumultuous place, this country of yours. PMI, sweetheart, would be not days or months, but years.'

'Yes, Enid dear, they are the Naxalites. Mostly Chamars, but many poor Jats too. They did not go on for long though. Wrote lovely songs while they lasted.' It must have been the intoxicating jasmine fragrance that prompted me to confide the secrets of my land to her.

The mummies kept coming, faster and faster, like shrivelled beams of coal.

'These are PMI fifty, hundred, thousand years, sweetheart. What do you have here? A river or a bloody Louvre of your own?'

'The Partition, Enid. The Partition of India. A million at one go. The work of our own artists helped by our friendly rulers, which were, at the time you guys, Enid, with all due respect. The even blacker ones are the works of Persians, Mongols, Greeks, and Afghans. This is the route invaders have taken since the beginning of time. Enid, this river of mine has been busy for thousands of years.'

Enticed by her fragrance, I leaned in to kiss her. But suddenly there was no jasmine, and it was the stale smell of Famous Grouse on her breath. I woke up with a start, my whole body drenched in sweat.

Thirteen

The Boys continued to have the upper hand; the policemen, even those with crooked fingers, were no match for them. With a carefree abandon, they went on bombing railway stations, derailing trains, making river bridges disappear in moments and killing by the hundred every month. TV channels in other parts of the country often used stock images from earlier tragedies to drive home a point and labelling it 'file' so you did not confuse it for a fresh happening. Not in P-3 though. Here, if a TV screen was showing a massacre, it had to have happened that day. No reruns, no lack of content in P-3. No 'file'.

The money, as I said, came from Grenada, the country of homesick Punjabis. Sikhs living in P-3 were tired of watching people die like flies in the so-called holy war being waged in their name, but some of their co-religionists in Grenada, secure in the safety of distance, played complex gurudwara politics. In the name of creating a separate country, they collected heaps of dollars, kept some, and sent the rest to the homeland. The people who died were both Hindus and Sikhs. The bombs that went off in crowded trains and busy markets were faultlessly secular.

The Boys escaped on motorcycles and in stolen cars into the Golden Temple, the holy mecca for Sikhs across the world. The police were not allowed to go there in pursuit, ostensibly not to hurt the sensibilities of the Sikhs of P-3, most of whom, by now had no love lost for the Boys.

That year, however, when an exceptionally hot summer was at its peak, Prime Minister Durga, in Delhi, lost her patience and ordered the army to march into the Golden Temple. The centuries-old crowded areas of the city around the temple were evacuated. The narrow lanes were widened with dynamite to make way for tanks. Heavy mortar shelling felled parts of the 400-year-old temple. The fiery Sikh priest, who was now the commander-in-chief of the insurrection with residence in the temple, was killed along with scores of his soldiers. Among those who perished as cannon fodder in the crossfire were hundreds of worshippers who were there because, well, it was a place of worship. And it happened to be around the day on which a Mughal emperor had executed a Sikh guru hundreds of years back; so, it was a special day of worship, and several times more worshippers than usual were there inside the temple. The army generals had simply forgotten that detail. If they remembered, they did not consider it important.

A curfew was imposed in the city. For days, after the army operation, the people of Amritsar were not allowed to go anywhere near the temple, because witnessing the damage would have provoked their anger even further. The artillery holes had made solid walls look like filigree and the hasty patchwork made things look worse.

'Collateral damage, unfortunately, could not be avoided,' the government spokeswoman in Delhi had said, looking right into the camera, with a straight face. Many bodies were not found. Many of those found could not be identified. For weeks, families would queue up at the row of rooms outside the temple where, worshippers had left their footwear before going in. Desperate men and women would go through the numbered slots, where pairs were kept in ones or twos or more. Before going into the room, they folded their hands and muttered a prayer, hoping not to find the pair of shoes or sandals or chappals they were looking for. But all of them did. And each time one was found, wails went up.

India, however, heaved a sigh of relief. Overnight, the nomenclature had changed. India now meant the country outside P-3. India, the aggressor, the bully, the bugger. Indians, however, were happy with Durga and were convinced that now that the nerve centre of terrorism had been vanquished by Durga, lasting peace would reign.

Sikhs living in the state of two and a half rivers, who so far had nothing against Durga, were horrified the moment tanks entered their sanctum. Each of them felt individually violated. It was argued that had the state been a separate country of Sikhs, this would have never happened. Maybe, the Boys did have a point after all, they said aloud to themselves.

The common Sikhs, men and women, Jats, Khatris, and Dalits left for Amritsar in processions of motorcycles, tractor trolleys, and jeeps fitted with loudspeakers, defying restrictions. They carried nothing but harmoniums, flutes, cymbals, and *chimtas* borrowed from gurudwaras. The small groups on dusty tracks merged to form long unending processions on all the roads leading to the smashed Golden Temple. They sang hymns of duty, dignity, and sacrifice to protect their honour. The countryside rang with *shabads* like '*Deh siva bar mohe* (Bless us to win or die fighting in the battle for the right)'—a battle song written by the scholar-warrior Guru Gobind Singh.

The processions were stopped at various places, short of Amritsar, by army trucks parked across roads. Those who did not turn back were fired at and more people died.

The hurt and humiliation was echoed by Sikhs around the world. An Indian ambassador in Europe resigned and turned an ideologue for the cause. An atheist Sikh writer returned his award. Some Sikh soldiers in the army turned mutinous and many deserted. Sikh boys in India, even those who were born elsewhere and had never been to P-3, started growing beards and learning how to tie turbans.

In the schools of P-3, overnight, one could make out Sikh students from Hindu students. Attendance in gurudwaras multiplied. People who were indifferent to the religion became devout.

The Sikhs shrank into the fortress of their identity and bolted the door shut.

Jeet would collect his milk bill every month on the seventh, but this time he seemed to have forgotten. Some months, that was the only time I saw him as the medications made me sleep till late and he came early. He had the key to the gate so he would come up to the kitchen and leave the milk in the small Kelvinator I now had.

That morning I set an early alarm and waited for his steps on the stairs.

When I came out with the money, he pulled the notes from my hand and turned to go. For the first time, he was wearing a turban neatly tied rather than just a *parna* wrapped around his head. He even had a moustache and short beard on his earlier clean-shaven face. I had to sprint down after him, because he did not turn back when I called.

At the bottom of the stairs, I pulled him around to face me, 'I did not attack the Golden Temple, did I?'

Jeet kept the empty vessel on the stairs, threw his arm and a half around me and sobbed like a child. With his one firm hand and the other soft stump, he clutched me against him and kept crying. Abruptly then, as if embarrassed, he let go of me, got on his cycle propped against the wall, and rode away. At the back of his cycle, he had got fitted a metal *khanda*, the Sikh emblem with two edged swords and a circle which, a patient had told me, symbolized 'Community, Sword, Victory'. For the first time in my life, standing there on the homeland of my ancestors, I felt excluded by the circumference of a steel circle and the swords around it.

Fourteen

About five months months later, in Delhi, a British film maker assigned to make a documentary on Durga's life had an appointment with her. Her office was next to a sprawling garden, which was a part of her house. That autumn morning, the garden was awash with white dahlias and pink chrysanthemums. As she crossed the garden to pass through the connecting wicker gate, two of her Sikh body guards— one of them a personal favourite for years, fired so many rounds into her that it took doctors a whole day just to count the number of bullets in the body.

TV anchors reported the news of the shooting several hours later: Sikh guards had shot the reigning prime minister, whom they were supposed to protect, just for doing her duty of saving the country from terrorists. The news of her death was delayed, but people knew anyway from the BBC radio.

Lessons needed to be taught, lessons which would not be forgotten in a hurry, Durga's ministers exhorted their minions around the country. For three subsequent days, Sikhs were hunted down the streets of Indian cities. They were killed and slaughtered by marauding mobs, who became increasingly creative on the job. Old tyres were hung around the victims' necks, petrol splashed, and match lit. The police were sent away on an unofficial vacation. They came back in plainclothes to lead the pogrom. The government supplied voters' lists to locate Sikh houses and shops, which were looted and then burnt. The open season on looting attracted more killers from villages around the cities.

Sikh army men on leave were dragged out of trains, stabbed, and left next to the tracks to die while the trains moved on.

For several years, the state had been burning and India had been calm. For days after Durga's death, India was burning and the state was seething, but was outwardly calm. It was the calm before the hurricane of revenge.

The thing about hurricanes of revenge is that each subsequent one is more vicious. The countryside, in those weeks, produced more Boys than ever before. They came up like mushrooms after a spell of overnight rain.

The eerie quiet was shattered one night by bombs going off in a colony meant for police officers, in the heart of the city. Those trying to escape were mowed down by automatic gunfire. Burning houses were searched and all service weapons taken away. It was the worst carnage so far, in years of what had been one horrific massacre after the other.

The state braced up for even worse. An emergency meeting of the top brass was held at a secret location and retaliation was planned. Even the pretence at following the rule of law was to be let go, the committee decided.

The only written minutes of that meeting reflected the decision to pass laws that would allow detention for years without trial, make confessions in police custody valid evidence in a court of law, and sanctioning of a budget to construct 10 more one-way Gaayab Saraks leading to 10 more Gyms. Even more modern equipment was ordered to service these centres of excellence. Since the earlier names evoked a wrong imagery in people's minds, the new Gaayab Saraks would be called Liberation Roads and the new Gyms, Rehabilitation Centres.

The new set-ups quickly gained such a reputation that men lifted away on suspicion of terrorism would bribe officers to send them to the old Gym rather than one of the new Rehab Centres, or RCs, as they came to be known. The RCs had the technology to deliver pain of calibrated intensity to specific areas of the human body, without producing any blood, gore, or even a scar, and without as much as touching the target site. An electrode cap was placed around the head and extremely specific areas of the brain stimulated by certain degrees. It was all precise and individualized.

The screams produced therein were silent, because the sound energy was recycled back to produce even more pain. That also discouraged screaming. The whole operation was so soundless that no soundproofing was needed. Some of the later RCs did not have any Liberation Roads leading to them and were embedded in busy marketplaces. A young couple in a posh restaurant could carry on their flirtatious banter without having an inkling that on the other side of the wall, less than two feet away from where they sat, a man was being subjected to 24-carat pure pain to his genitalia. Instead, the young man who lived in Delhi and had come by the morning train to meet his girlfriend, said, 'This place is so peaceful, so normal. My mom was needlessly worried.'

Information forced out of the silent suspects was picked up by sensitive sensors directly from their vocal cords. It was printed on reams of paper slithering out of silent machines, which folded the paper neatly upon itself in a tray, and printed the name of the source, interrogator, and date and time of the session. These documents—the Maai-baaps could read at leisure in the evening. The death of suspects was inevitable, because the exquisite pain was hard on the hearts of even the young men.

The chess players of Grenada sensed a check mate was in sight. A city newspaper on their payroll carried advice to Hindu brothers that the time to say good-bye had come and, if the lessons learnt from the Partition were anything to go by, it would be dangerous to delay the departure till the end. The chess players sent even more money and made even more phone calls.

Pages torn out of the holy Sikh book were found in front of a busy gurudwara and rumours went around blaming Hindus. To underline the point, a well-known Hindu trader was shot dead in the city square the following morning. The gurudwara priests, all seasoned old men, however, went about the task of quietly restoring the dignity of the scripture without blaming anyone, because the assassinated Hindu man, for years, had been a regular donor to the gurudwara. His eldest son had been raised a Sikh.

The tail of a cow was cut off and thrown in front of the hundred-year-old Kali temple in the city. It was meant to terrorize Hindus who worshipped cows. When a man was sent to the temple the next morning to assess the impact, he was surprised to find it full of noisy medical students—boys and girls, Hindus and Sikhs—whose final examination was to start in two hours. They were there to bribe the goddess with offerings, as generations of medical students had done before them. The dismembered tail had been found on the marble stairs of the temple at 3 in the morning. It had been buried by the old priest ritually, but quietly.

The insurrection was getting out of the state's hands. The vast triangle of area further down the river, where the Beas joined the Satluj, was virtually a separate state already. *The Indian Express*, which I had started subscribing to, was brought for me by Jeet along with the milk. The news, one winter morning, read something like this:

'The ubiquitous *sarkanda* (elephant grass), overrunning the marshy river islands, lush green fields, and meadows of the picturesque Mand, is symbolic of its people— mostly Kamboj and Rai Sikhs. The stiff and stubborn grass regenerates stronger the more one tries to destroy it by fire or sickle.

Equally obdurate are the people of the Mand. Spread over 600 square kilometres of the riverine areas of four districts, they nonchalantly weather the worst. High floods are just another season, and the fight against nature, a way of life. Between the annual floods that wash away lush green fields in a matter of hours, they specialize in stealing paddy or the wheat crop. Terrorism, breeding relentlessly in the Mand is no different, for it has only grown through the five war-scale flushing out operations conducted by the paramilitary forces... The result is that from once being a safe hide-out, the Mand has now become the headquarters for the killer gangs.'

When things seemed to be going completely out of hand, the Centre dismissed the State government in exile and Delhi took over direct control.

Fifteen

The old Gym, in the rear of the Gurukul, as it was now being called to distinguish it from the ultra-modern rehab centres embedded in community spaces, much like the primary health centres and post offices, continued to function at full capacity. And there was nothing old about it; it was just folk terminology. It had been repainted, both inside and outside, and the one-way soundproof glass in front was replaced with even more effective soundproof glass. It had even newer technology, most of which was still unpacked, because the staff were more comfortable with the earlier machines which were quite efficient anyway. The rear gate of the Gurukul now had watchtowers, manned day and night by gunmen. Jeeps came with young men and left without them. Sometimes, there were buses that came, those that had been appropriated from private transporters and modified to suit the purpose.

Information retrieved from men was stored and the bodies sent to the incinerator. The ashes were mixed in the soil of the hundred acres of land newly bought for the Gym. This patch of land was to grow food for the staff mess, visitors' canteen, and domestic kitchens of the Gurukul, which itself was now twice its earlier size and a deemed university to boot. The degrees granted at the convocation were signed by the vice-chancellor, who was also the director of Gurukul. The Gurukul even received an award from the National University Commission for outstanding research in the field of community outreach. The gardeners and the older officers interested in and knowledgeable about gardening—and there were many such aficionados—were dumbfounded one morning. The wheat fields were full of tall sunflower plants jostling for space with wheat stalks and winning. The old gardener, who had a sub-inspector rank, swore that he had not sown even a single sunflower seed. The plants had just sprung up overnight. The hundred acres spread of the deep yellow flowers swaying in the morning breeze flummoxed the helicopter pilot who had brought the 'Maai-baap *ke* Maai-baap', 'MB Square' for short, from the capital-in-exile to inaugurate another research wing at the Gurukul. Adding to his confusion was the fact that, instead of facing the sun, the sunflowers stubbornly faced the west, away from the Gym.

That the new Gyms and RCs were effective was unquestionable. The zeal with which they were run, however, often made them far too effective. A man who has an electronic probe activating the pain centre in his brain or, in the case of the old Gym, is subjected to an overweight policeman sitting on each end of a roller balanced on his thighs, knows soon enough that it is information in the form of names and addresses that will ease his pain, if only for a short while. So, names and addresses were given. Any names and matching addresses would do, but the people had to be real, since their existence could be confirmed by the police within minutes and, if it was found that those people did not exist, the inspector would bring even worse pain.

The man who regurgitated the names would be ashes in a few hours since, at some point, he would run out of verifiable names and addresses. But the men he named would be brought in on account of what was called in files, 'actionable intelligence'. After a few hours in the Gym, these men would confess to any shooting, massacre, or bombing, and, in turn, name *their* 'collaborators'. So, the cycle went on.

To say that seasoned interrogators could not tell apart the innocent from the guilty would be an insult their expertise. However, the government, meanwhile, had started a new scheme of cash awards to incentivize the overworked officers. These awards were contingent upon numbers, and that made it difficult for officers (who had crooked fingers to begin with) to send back clients, just because they seemed innocent. Remember, all the officers with straight fingers— who constituted a fairly large number, in fact, a majority, whatever the cynics may say—were still languishing in administrative assignments. Their association, OSF (officers with straight fingers), had, several times, requested the government to be put on operational duties. Each time, they were reminded of their failure in the past to retrieve even an ounce of ghee from the can, when they had the chance. Now that the job was finally being done, they were advised not to let their narcissism jeopardize national interest. After all, sometimes, the end is more important than the means. If these officers were still unhappy, they were welcome to resign and join Amnesty International or wherever officers with straight fingers went after leaving their jobs. This was the gist of what the tall and thin Sikh police chief with curled moustache conveyed stiffly to the delegation of officers with straight fingers.

Somewhere along the line, after some months, the goings-on at the Gym and RCs got not just derailed, but turned entirely into a macabre farce. The incentives lay in numbers. How could anybody, even a crack police force with a decade of counterinsurgency experience bring forward real terrorists in those numbers every day, even if they happened to be there. Inevitably, there were days when only innocent men were brought in and confabulated intelligence recorded. The real terrorists continued to wreak real terror. Money from Grenada kept pouring in and arms from across the border kept being purchased. The terrorists now had even better automatic guns, which fired hundreds of rounds in a minute. There were bombs which looked like tiffin boxes, cameras, and transistors—tiffin boxes, which carried real parathas and pickle; cameras, which took real pictures; and transistors, which relayed real music and breaking news, the latter sometimes even before an event occurred. 'Hundred and twenty people will be killed, at the end of this bulletin, at the bustling fair along the canal where Chhat Pooja is being celebrated.' The news always proved to be true. Even the numbers, give or take a few.

Sometimes, money from Grenada did not reach in time, or the bursars kept a larger than usual portion for themselves. When you collect millions of dollars for funding an armed rebellion in another country, nobody expects you to keep ledgers.

To tide over cash flow issues, the Boys started kidnapping rich men for ransom. A successful businessman or a famous architect or a hotshot cardiologist would be accosted on his way to work, blindfolded, gagged, and driven away in a car without a number plate, all in full public view. Typically, this person, whose religion did not matter, only riches did, would be made to walk for hours in the thistly Mand to a remote safe house. The family would be informed once the catch was safely deposited and could not be traced. Ransom money was quick to come, there was no bargaining, the panic-stricken family eager to know how soon they could bring the money and where. The police were never informed. The police knew of course, since the men were snatched away in broad daylight on busy streets, sometimes dramatically in front of traffic policemen, which was all deliberate because the terror unleashed was what made the next operation and the ransom payment even smoother. After the transaction was completed, newspapers issued an official statement owning up the act on the letterhead of the Liberation Force, and the exact amount of ransom received with thanks.

Once the released man reached home, with feet swollen from walking through the fields the whole night, he sometimes found men from the income tax department waiting for him. These men had read the newspaper and were curious about the source of this ransom money that had not been declared to the tax authorities.

Soon the Boys discovered that kidnapping schoolgoing children of the very rich was a simpler operation, more remunerative, and the money came in even faster.

With so much quick money to be made, it was only a matter of time before the real professionals decided to reclaim their game. The groundwork had already been done for them by terrorists. The air was thick with all-pervasive fear. All that the professional kidnapper had to do was to print the stationery of the dreaded fighter forces. The kidnappers already had the guns. Soon it became difficult to know whether a child had been kidnapped by holy fighters or unholy criminals. Not that it mattered to the families. Both killed if they were not paid. There was no point in trying to find out if their son or father or husband had been kidnapped by this or that commando force or by professional gangs. However, the competition hampered the purists' business. The hardened criminals tortured their victims and, sometimes, killed them even after receiving the ransom. Kidnapping was easy, but to return the kidnapped person ran the risk of alerting the police of their whereabouts. But everyone believed the killing of the kidnapped person even after receiving the ransom was the Boys' doing since the ransom note had come written on their letter head, which looked genuine enough. Thanks to the professionals, the Boys were fast losing the moral high ground, which was the only currency they had other than fear. The kidnapper gangs diversified into assassinating business rivals for money and pinned it on the Boys. They made it look so much like a terrorist killing that the police would do a cursory investigation and throw their hands up.

You wanted a business competitor dead. Fine. Pay the gang 20 lakh rupees, half now and half later. Your adversary would receive an extortion letter on the letterhead of the Liberation Army demanding 40 lakh rupees. He would bargain a deal for 25 and pay 10 as advance to the turbaned young man who came into his drawing room on a frosty morning. Confident that a deal had been struck, the man went for his usual stroll in the park where he would be shot.

The family would receive a phone call in a gruff voice, 'Come and pick up your husband. He is lying dead in the park. We asked for 40 lakh rupees, he gave us 10. This is what comes out of short-changing holy warriors of the Liberation Army. Victory to the Cause!' The police looked at the letter, talked to the maid who had seen the young turbaned man and closed the case as yet another terrorist killing. The truth of the matter was that the Liberation Army knew nothing about it. The criminals collected 20 lakhs from you, 10 from the victim, your work was accomplished as promised, and the Liberation Army who knew nothing about it got the bad name.

After the attack on the Golden Temple, many youngsters had joined the liberation movement. Several of them came from wealthy Jat families. Young boys love guns and the power that comes with them. And, of course, the glamour. The glamour tended to wear off rather quickly, as the harsh, spartan life and fear of torture unnerved those who had grown up in comfort. Going home was not an option though. The police would kill them with their 'no prisoners' policy. Many of them surrendered with their weapons and sought to make a deal with the police. 'Keep us alive and safe and we will work for you. We are trained fighters. Nobody knows your enemy better than us, because until this morning, *we* were your enemy. The government raised a whole cadre of such ex-Boys. On their own request, they were kept in the jails for minor offences, as trivial as carrying an unlicensed revolver. These ex-Boys went and killed the current Boys during the night and returned to jail the next morning on their own. Ironically, their jail cells were the only place they felt safe in. For some reason, they came to be known as the Black Cats or just Cats.

There were areas where groups of policemen had been killed while patrolling at night. When this happened repeatedly, policemen simply refused to go there. It was the Black Cats, then, who were sent to those hotspots. Some of them were also killed, but others managed to assert themselves more dominantly, on behalf of the police. The problem with hiring rogue soldiers, however, is that they can go rogue again. The Cats soon got into the habit of entering the houses of the rich at night, wearing their brand-new police uniform and carrying police weapons. They not only robbed their jewellery, but also raped the women. The police would claim the next morning that this was the handiwork of the Boys dressed as policemen which was, in a way, true. Black Cats defiled the image of the holy fighters like nothing else could.

By now, there were multiple stakeholders in the field. In addition to the original rivals, the freedom fighters, and the police, there were criminals, who worked as hired assassins and kidnapped for ransom, and there were Black Cats, who had state protection and arms issued by the government. The Cats could never be prosecuted for those crimes. Remember, they were all supposed to have been in jail at the time of those robberies and rapes.

Sixteen

The Boys, with the sole purpose of refurbishing their holier than thou image, issued a slew of firmans to ensure piety in people's lives. Women were to wear a plain chunni and cover their heads. They were prohibited from wearing bindis, saris, and glass bangles and from observing fast on *karva chauth*. All these were supposed to be Hindu symbols and customs, according to the firman handwritten in Gurumukhi, copies of which were found pasted all over the state one morning. The firmans were idiosyncratic, but were issued in the name of a 'Council' to lend an impression of consensus to these.

To drive home the point more tellingly, two college girls in jeans were kidnapped from a busy road outside their college by a bunch of car-borne Boys wearing white robes and blue turbans. The girls were found, two hours later, at the same spot from where they were kidnapped, wearing white salwar kameez, with their heads demurely covered. They had been taken to a nearby house, slapped around, forced to change clothes, and duly deposited back.

The religious right often finds itself intertwined with the social left. The Boys fixed doctors' fees at 50 rupees and monthly school fees at 200 rupees according to another firman, firmans having become a regular feature anticipated with trepidation by people. Another *hukamnama* made an appearance three days later, photocopies of which were found pasted on walls of post offices, railway stations, on the sides of roadway buses, and under the wipers of parked cars across the state. It decreed that all ostentation at weddings was to be done away with. Sikh weddings were to be simple religious ceremonies, to be performed in gurudwaras, not in hotels or homes. There was to be no drinking or dancing, even afterwards. To underline the seriousness of the Council's intent, members of a wedding orchestra, including its band members and dancing girls, were viciously attacked at 4 in the morning when their canter was waiting at a railway crossing for the train to pass. Two dancers in their finery, two bhangra boys, and three band boys and their driver were shot at close range. Their trombones and the rest of the musical instruments were found crushed flat on the railway line after the train had passed.

So accustomed Shamsie was to working at night that she continued to sleep during the day and taking a shower in the evening. She would then get ready in a pair of jeans and a shirt, make herself a drink and sit in front of the second-hand colour TV that they had bought from their neighbours. The neighbours had moved to Faridabad, after their younger son was killed in the bombing at Gulab Theatre, where he worked as an usher.

Dhakka Colony, the inhabitants of which went to work at night and slept during the day, found its rhythm flattened. There were no late-night parties in restaurants. The waiters and dancers were out of work, and there were no auto rickshaws waiting at the bus stop in the evenings. The hookers were the only ones who still had work. But the sleek cars waiting for them at discrete corners had disappeared. The girls now went out, dressed in modest salwar-kameez, with their heads covered, and preferred to walk across the road into the city lanes after dark. As more and more dancers got bored and ran out of money, they joined the hookers. The oldest profession not just survived, but swelled in ranks, because the men in the city were bored too with nothing to do at nights. College boys coined a ditty, 'Dhakka Colony, bread is steep, but the whores are cheap.'

As she sipped her drink, Shamsie realized that she could not go out in her jeans without being kidnapped. If she were seen drinking, she would be shot. She watched mechanically as gory scenes of a train bombing were being shown on TV; each image showed bleeding and crying victims being carried away from the derailed coach. She was horrified when she realized how all of it felt so mundane to her.

The orchestra had been getting a lot of work over the year before the dictate, and the two had rented a small apartment on a first floor. Bheem was the one who had insisted upon the change. She had gone along, after hesitating for a while. Maybe, she had had an intuition. Maybe, she was more pragmatic than Bheem, when it came to money matters. Bheem did not particularly care about saving. Just like when he was a child, and had spent the entire 5 rupees he stole from Master Batta on jalebis. They were earning more and had hired three more girls to cater to daytime functions. The audience was less demanding at that hour. 'You work so hard and all through the night. You need a quieter place to sleep during the day,' Bheem had said.

Shamsie thought that she saw Bheem's face for a moment on the TV screen and shot up in her chair. It was only a fleeting glimpse, and she thought that maybe, it was the alcohol making her see things. But she was not even halfway through her drink. To placate herself, Shamsie rationalized... there was no reason for Bheem to have been on a train.

Bheem had removed the stickers from his scooter, but he still went to see his comrade friends from his marketing days in the villages.

'What is the point of meeting people when we are not performing? Can't you spend a few waking hours just with me?' Shamsie had complained. She did not say that she was mortally scared of him going out. Nevertheless, he should have known. Just two days ago, another bhangra dancer had been killed in a market for being an orchestra worker. He was not even performing; he had come to buy vegetables.

'Waking hours sure, but you sleep till lunch. I will be back by then.' But Bheem had not returned.

Shamsie kept her glass at a distance and focused on the TV, her eyes glued to the screen. There he was again, the front of his shirt full of blood. Two men carrying an unconscious woman blocked the view just then. She was bleeding so much that it seemed her naval was spouting blood. Once they passed, Shamsie saw Bheem again. This time, the camera lingered on his face, and she saw him carrying a child lying still in his arms.

She was taken aback on seeing Bheem standing at the door just then. It took her a minute to realize that it was him standing there even as she could see him on TV, carrying a dead child. The blood on his shirt had dried. She clung to him; she was shivering so much that he had to hold her tight. His scooter would not start, the plug had broken, he had left it with a mechanic near the railway station and had taken the train, he explained while patting her back.

Bheem went into the bathroom, and took some time washing himself. When he came out, he sat quietly for a long time. Just like he would on the canal bridge as a young boy, after his mother had died.

After failing to remove the blood from his shirt, Shamsie returned from the bathroom and insisted there was nothing else to do other than to go back to Bombay and give it another try. If it meant dancing in bars for her, so be it.

Bheem thought that they should wait. Nothing new had happened. Trains had been blown up before. He wanted them to work at some other jobs till the Boys found something else to do and forgot about dancers. He could get a job in a security agency. Shamsie could work as a receptionist in an office. This led to their second fight in a week.

'You and your canals will get us both killed,' Shamsie blurted.

'You and your dance will exile us for ever.'

Bheem pretended he was not rattled, but he was. More than he had ever been. It was not the whole compartment exploding into pieces that shook him. Not even the trunkless limbs lying around or the deafening shrieks and crying. It was the whimpering child he had carried, who soon went limp in his arms.

Bheem suddenly stopped arguing, clung to Shamsie, and lay quietly. They agreed to sleep over the matter and to talk to Sidhu in the morning.

Sidhu tried to argue on Bheem's behalf, but his arguments were not convincing, even to himself. As a last ditch attempt, the three went to Ambala to explore the city with the intention of settling down there. Ambala was two hours away and not in P-3. Hence, safe. Since it was just an overgrown garrison town, they expected rents to be affordable. It turned out to be four times more than what they could pay.

'Because of the Punjab problem, madam. It is the first town as you come out of Punjab and Punjabi refugees are rich refugees. They have driven up the rents. That is what they did at the time of partition also, my father tells me.'

That day, they got the phone disconnected and closed the office down. Most of the offices in the building were already shuttered up. But nobody sold or rented out since, like Bheem, they glibly rationalized that the Punjab 'problem' was bound to solve itself sooner or later. There was no logic to this assessment. But then again, there was no logic to any of what had been happening for nearly a decade now.

Sidhu's father told him that was what he had thought when giving the keys of his Sialkot house to his neighbours at the time of Partition. That he would come back and reclaim his house. But the border kept burning for months and he could not go back. Meanwhile, the house, he heard, had been allotted to a Muslim family from India.

Sidhu came to see them off at the station, even though the train left at midnight and his village was an hour away on a road that was unsafe at night during the best of times. As the Frontier Mail entered the station, it was packed to the full with passengers standing on footboards. It reminded Shamsie of the black and white cover of a book on Partition that she had seen years ago. Lying on an upper berth, she remembered the leathery face and shrewd eyes of the property agent in Ambala. The loud clickety clack of the train through the open window sounded to her as 'refugees, refugees'. Two hours later, from the deep cacophony that trains produce when crossing a bridge, she knew the train was crossing over Ghaggar River, which was where P-3 ended. It was only then that she could sleep.

On the lower berth, Bheem waited for the booming sound of the train crossing first, the Bhakra canal bridge near their village, where he and Shamsie had swum most summer afternoons as kids, and then, the bridge on the Ghaggar. He should have felt a sense of relief after this crossing. But unlike Shamsie, he did not relax. He just remembered Sidhu's father, who could never go back. When Shamsie woke up, the train was at a standstill at the Delhi railway station. She saw Bheem jostle with crowds at the compartment door, balancing plastic cups of tea over people's heads.

Shamsie spent a week trying to get an assistant's job at the dancing school in Andheri where she had trained. The job involved organizing logistics, locating and tuning instruments, adjusting and preparing schedules, and informing trainees whenever there were changes. She was eventually told that they would have liked to hire her, but since there was no vacancy right then, she could leave a phone number instead. She gave the number of the dance bar where Bheem had started work. Unknown to her, the school had called there two months later. On finding that it was a dance bar and Shamsie, a bar dancer, they had disconnected the phone in a hurry.

Ironically, the name of the bar was Roshni Punjab Bar. It was owned by an 80-year-old sprightly Sardarji born in Jalandhar, who looked like a bird with an outsized turban. The dances were on the beats and tunes Shamsie was accustomed to. Salaries were good. There was an option to stay in the same building, on the top floor. It was convenient to change into costume, apply makeup, and take the lift down to work. And yet, after a week or so, they started to feel cooped up, Bheem more so. He was already missing the open fields. Somebody suggested a room in Indira Nagar, a few minutes away. It was a slum, but the front was a row of newly built one-room tenements with balconies.

It took away half their income, but that was not bad by Bombay standards.

Two weeks later, Shamsie started to wonder if Bheem had been right and whether they had jumped the gun in leaving in a hurry. They talked about it, but Bheem never said 'I told you so'. In fact, now that they were in Bombay, he was better at trying to fit in. It was also easier for him, since he had the same job as before. Monday, Wednesday, Thursday, and Friday nights he would stand in a safari suit at one corner of the dance floor from 8 in the evening till 3 in the morning. Most nights, his mere presence was enough, he did not have to do anything. Sometimes, a cold stare, a nudge towards a chair, or escorting a drunk man outside and finding him a taxi was what was required. Saturdays were rough. More men came, and they drank more. Bheem, along with three others, stood outside the entrance to keep an eye out for known troublemakers. On Tuesdays, the place was closed.

Shamsie knew the routine of a dance bar well, she had lived inside one before. But certain things had changed. Clients were now allowed to dance with the girls and, after a couple of drinks, most men wanted to. Shamsie was accustomed to dancing on a wide-open stage, with the audience at a distance and at a lower plane. And here in the dance bar, the dancing was just a come-hither swaying. That the men were clumsy and did not know how to dance was besides the point. The new business policy was that drunk men were allowed to dance and the girls encouraged to be seductive, while keeping a distance. Shamsie was the only girl whose boyfriend also worked there. Sardarji did not know what to do with her. He did not expect her to be flirtatious with clients when Bheem stood 10 feet away. Maybe they were even married and had preferred not to say since dance bars hired only single women. However, good bouncers, who did not drink at work, were difficult to find, and Bheem came highly recommended by his previous employer, Sardarji's friend, who ran a bar in Kurla. Bheem had insisted he would join only if Shamsie was hired too. The Sardarji knew all about the fires raging in his home state. Two of his brothers still lived there with their families. After seeing Shamsie dance, he decided her talent was wasted in a dance bar. The old man offered her the job of an office assistant to help him run the place.

This worked well for Bheem and Shamsie who now had the whole afternoon to themselves. Shamsie furnished her home with cane furniture from the nearby Chembur Camp. The window faced east and, since mornings were the only time they could sleep, Shamsie put up dark curtains bought from the shop of good-natured Sharma, a friend of Sardarji. They were slowly building up a network of acquaintances. Their old scooter was upgraded to a new Rajdoot motor bike and they bought a refrigerator. On Tuesdays, they went to Khandala, Elephanta, and even the Vasai Fort. Shamsie bought colourful lanterns from Kolaba for Diwali, which was still a month away. For the first time ever, there was space for a 4-feet-wide bed. All through, they had only a single bed in their room and a camp cot, which would lie folded and stored under the bed during the day.

'Are you sure?' asked Bheem, after they had finished their early dinner at breakfast time.

'No, I am not. But there is place, so you might as well sleep here,' she had said kissing the mole on his leg by which he told right from left.

The Sardarji was a talkative man. One night, after a couple of drinks from the bottle of Red Label he kept hidden behind the ledgers, he said to Shamsie, 'Not that it is any of my business, but since you are a Punjabi, maybe I can ask… Why don't you two get married and have a baby?'

He wondered if that came out a little abrupt. 'Unless, of course, you do not want to do it ever, which is also fine. I mean, this is as good a time as any. I can even think of appointing Bheem as manager. He is a good boy, polite, serious, not gossipy—that is good for this business. I might even get to retire. My wife and I can finally live in the cottage we have in Khandala. My son is in Pune and we could spend more time with our grandsons. I will be happy if a Punjabi is in charge when I am not here. If I must be cheated by someone, I would rather he be a Punjabi.'

She was perplexed at Bheem's reluctance. 'This is too much of a responsibility. There are huge amounts of money involved, a lot of it is off the books. The cashier may pilfer, and then, I will be held responsible. The girls are difficult to manage. Their boyfriends come and start quarrels about their wages…"Seema gets more, why should Ruhi get less…".' Here, he did a good imitation of Ruhi's Tamil trans boyfriend, who was the muscleman of a Kurla don. 'The worst are the policemen, who come to gawk at girls and guzzle free beer. And demand more and more money each week.'

Shamsie did not interrupt. She knew that these things he could manage, that there had to be more to his hesitation. And there was.

'I do not want to get too used to this place. I do not want to take this on and then suddenly decide to go back, once things are better there.'

They had been reading newspapers, watching TV, and discussing with Sardarji, who, in turn, talked to his brothers in Jalandhar every afternoon before coming to work. The overwhelming consensus was that things would never get better. The bombs, kidnappings, and rapes had only multiplied. A senior police officer had been kidnapped from his fortified office. Four terrorist commanders, who had been arrested a day before, were released in exchange for him.

Terrorism and regular crime had become intertwined in public perception. On a typical day, the ideologues issued statements owning up the bomb blasts and slayings of brick-kiln workers from Bihar, but distancing themselves from the rape of a schoolgirl. 'Yes, we kidnapped the industrialist father-son duo for the holy cause, but, no, we were not the ones who robbed their neighbour's house and raped the daughter-in-law.'

Then came news from Jalandhar that Sardarji's two brothers, along with their large families, had moved to Faridabad, near Delhi. The factory that their father and uncles had built brick by brick, after losing everything in

Lahore during the partition, had been set ablaze, after an impossible extortion demand by the Liberation Force could not be met. The insurers had washed their hands off saying that the policy did not cover damage resulting from an armed insurgency. They would go bankrupt if they started paying for all the damage the Boys had caused.

'And that is the place you are saving yourself for? People are fleeing from that inferno, and you want to go back into it?' Shamsie asked, slapping the breakfast plate on the table.

'That is not *a place*. That is home,' he had resented. After coming back to Bombay, for the first time, there was a shadow of another rift between the two. It was Bheem who stepped back and agreed to think about it.

A week later, Bheem was appointed manager of Roshni Punjab Dance Bar, at twice his previous salary, and Sardarji, with his wife, moved to Khandala for his much-delayed retirement.

Bheem turned out to be a rather skilful manager. Roshni Bar became a less noisy place. The cashier box was now fitted with a camera that streamed a live feed to the manager's office. The entry fee, which had so far been nominal, was increased several folds. It was adjustable against the cost of beer, but not refundable, thus keeping out the stragglers who came in just to watch. Bheem went to meet the police officer who was paid a weekly allowance. He offered to increase it by a half, if the officer ensured that the beat inspector and his men stayed away. The bar girls were given a 10 per cent raise on the strict condition that their boyfriends would not enter the premises. Shamsie improved the girls' dancing skills several notches. Initially, Sardarji would call every day to keep a check. As collections increased, his phone calls decreased.

As for the personal bit of advice from Sardarji, it kept hovering in the air. In any case, things were so picture perfect that they were wary of any change...until things were changed for them once again; this time, courtesy the Maratha Army.

The Maratha Army, notwithstanding the name, was a political party that whipped up parochial passions by villainizing people from outside the state as having cornered all the jobs, professions, and businesses in Bombay. At one stage, the party supremo, a self-professed Hitler admirer, had advocated a visa system for people from the rest of the country who wanted to come to Bombay. There were periodical drives, mostly before elections, during which the party goons would rough up taxi drivers from Bihar, hawkers from Uttar Pradesh, shopkeepers from the south of India, and taxi drivers from Punjab. The government never stopped them, because the Maratha Army would be in a loose alliance with one or the other of the major political parties, which ran the state at various periods in those times. The party also held itself up as a custodian of ancient Hindu heritage and its supposed purity of conduct. It was just a matter of time till the dance bars became the target, caught in the cross hairs of the Maratha Chief's telescopic gaze. Many of the dance bars belonged to South Indians and most bar girls, or bar *baalas* as they were called, were from states other than Maharashtra.

As the first step, the party came out with an editorial in its own newspaper, highlighting the evils of prostitution, alleging that dance bars were just pick-up places masquerading as bars. Dance bars were projected as immoral dens of prostitution, posing a danger to a society steeped in five thousand years of ascetic morality.

Sociologists argued in newspaper columns and on talk shows that dance bars were, in fact, a buffer against prostitution, and banning these would force the girls into actual prostitution. Since that was never the real issue anyway, the party persisted and even escalated its drive of spreading moral panic.

Sardarji happened to be the president of the Association of Dance Bars. He rushed from Khandala to appear in a TV debate and tried his best to defend against the seductive narrative of poor wives waiting at home and families being destroyed, with a rational, but by then staid, argument of adult choices and the opportunity of employment for thousands of girls working in dance bars across Bombay.

Right after the TV appearance by Sardarji, Roshni Dance Bar was pelted with stones. Three girls were injured, hit by shards of glass from the shattered windows. Shamsie received a cut above her eyebrow, which required two stitches and would leave a scar. The members of the Association of Dance Bars (the bar owners) decided to close their establishments for a while and gave paid leave to the girls. What the terrorists did, a thousand miles away, through handwritten posters pasted in the dead of the night, a bona-fide political party did here in broad daylight. After all, the Maratha Army could not be blamed if common people angered by depraved practices repugnant to their ancient culture threw a few stones, their mouthpiece pamphlet said in an editorial.

Within two weeks, things at the bars returned to normal as the political cyclone passed and the party workers diverted their attention to mutton shops that were rumoured to be selling beef on the side. The mutton shops were owned by Muslims, whom the party Chief called Pakistanis who needed to be shipped to Pakistan en masse. Yet, the political potential of the dance bar issue did not go unnoticed by the ruling party. Prompted by serious anti-incumbency sentiments threatening to overshadow the next assembly election a year away, there started earnest discussions within the cabinet about passing a new law banning the dance bars, thus hijacking the issue from the Maratha Army. This was eventually done some years later by another government.

Meanwhile, Bheem and Shamsie, who did not understand local politics, were shaken up not by the actual injury, but at being labelled 'outsiders'. Shamsie wondered how long one had to stay till one would not be called that. Bheem replied they would always be outsiders except in Punjab. Sidhu, who had followed the news, called every day. He thought he had a solution to their problem. He even thought he had found a sanctuary and jobs for them.

P-3 had scores of religious *deras* scattered all over the countryside, owned by one or the other sect, each headed by a man considered a demi-god by his followers. They congregated every Sunday, clogging the roads all over the state with traffic while going to prayer meetings addressed by one or the other prophet, who would be the descendant of an earlier prophet. Many followers lived in the campuses in accommodations built out of generous donations. Some of the larger *deras* were self-sufficient townships with secure perimeters and their own schools and hospitals. A few of these *deras* were populated, dominated, and even headed by Dalits. As Sidhu explained over his numerous telephone calls, although a large majority of militants were Jats, there were many Mazhabi Sikhs too from the lower castes. Even the Jat fighters came from families of marginal farmers, not from rich families with large landholdings. There were some Khatri Sikhs too from trading families in towns. Both as a matter of strategy and as a recognition of Dalit Sikhs' participation in the armed struggle, the Dalit *deras* and their ecosystems were left alone. They were safe sanctuaries in a state ravaged by war. This was despite a major irritant that followers of all *deras*, including Dalit ones, worshipped a living Guru, an anathema to the basic tenet of Sikhism that strictly upheld Guru Granth Sahib as being the last guru.

Sidhu had met people and found that one of the largest *deras* of those times, Dera Garibparvar, had several openings for security guards. They even had a job for a dance teacher in their newly-opened girl's school. All jobs in the security department at Dera Garibparvar were reserved for Dalits.

'This is tailor-made for you two,' he had gushed, 'I could even get a recommendation from a Dalit MLA for jobs and campus housing.'

'We would still have to go out for groceries and things,' Shamsie reminded Sidhu. 'Not if you do not want to. The place is like a city. It has a shopping centre, bank, post office, even its own railway station.'

Bheem was more determined of the two about not wanting to stay in Bombay a day longer than necessary. Shamsie suspected that, horrific as the incident of stone pelting had been, Bheem had used it as an opportunity to go back to his blessed canals and mustard fields. She also suspected Bheem had put Sidhu up to all the research. And she was right about that. However, this time she just went along.

Seventeen

My mood had been waxing and waning like the water level in Satluj. There were days when I had to go up to my terrace to locate the thin line of water bisecting the arid desert of the vast riverbed. Then, barely a month later, swirling waters would submerge most of the mound on which my house stood, waves lapping at my backyard. Sometimes, the river would swell up during winters too, when all one could see was dense fog beyond the windowpanes, shrouding the river, which you just knew was there. During such days, the house could not be seen even from the road, which itself was covered in opaque white. The fog would enter my head too and I would sit for hours waiting for a patient, oscillating between wanting and not wanting one to come. Not that it was easy to reach my house in that white miasma.

That morning, around 10 or 11, I heard a motorcycle and stiffened. Motorcycles were bad news. Scooters not so much. There was the sound of the gate being unlatched and of rubber on the gravel. The door was pushed open and there, against the wall of fog, stood Shamsie and Bheem at the door. The last time I had met them was with their entourage, on that morning while it was still dark, when Shamsie had smelt of vodka and was as high as a kite. This time, she hugged me in a distracted manner. She started telling me about their time in Bombay, and only then I realized that they had been away, so lost had I been within myself. She told me about the Boys' edict prohibiting dancing, the train Bheem had taken because his scooter would not start, the train which had been blown up, Roshni Punjabi Bar and the Sardarji from Jalandhar, their one room house in Chembur, and the ban on dance bars.

They had reached early morning by the Frontier Mail and had taken out just the motor bike from their luggage, deposited the rest in the cloakroom at the railway station, and come to meet me.

'So, here we are back like bad coins, once again,' she said. Bheem had gone to the terrace.

'He could have smoked here,' I said.

'He has gone to watch the fog over the river before it disappears. That is one reason he came back,' she explained on his behalf. 'And, I guess, to sing. He quit smoking. I started. Could I have one of yours?'

I got her my pack and an ashtray. She lit one like a regular and inhaled long and proper, not like some girls who took short puffs without inhaling and blew out a lot of smoke. I asked her about her past illness. If her disorder had worsened, she would have probably called me. Blowing a perfect circle, she told me she did not have fits anymore. She continued to experience momentary visions, but they were rare and did not bother her. She believed those were unrelated to any illness. For the few seconds they happened, she felt like she was part of another world, dancing a slow and languid dance on a music she had not heard anywhere else. 'I will call you if I need you. Meanwhile, let us give it a rest.' I got the message; my medical duties as far as she was concerned were over. It was not as abrupt as that, I just felt it was, in my bristly state of mind.

She crushed the cigarette in the ashtray and got up to open the window. Swirling fog billowed in and made the room damp. She was dressed for travel: in a salwar kameez, a loose sweater, and a pair of Nike sneakers, which looked original. She also had a small rhombus of a kundan pendant on a thin gold chain around her neck. It reminded me of my mother who had a similar thing, which I used to nuzzle against even when I was 12 years old.

'You look well,' I ventured in an attempt to normalize my mind.

'You don't,' she answered. 'Is something wrong?'

Well, that was not what I had expected.

We had never talked about me and I did not wish to start now. I was supposed to be the doctor and she, the patient, at least till now. Anyway, I was the last thing I wanted to talk about. Those days, I was in a shell within a shell. The thick layer of winter depression was an extra barricade around the walls of self-imposed seclusion and an effective one. Depression makes people grouchy. What business has this chit of a girl, less than half my age, going all maternal on me is what I thought. I had ring-fenced my mind, as if it were some blessed diamond people wanted to take away. There is a grandiosity of sorts in depression.

However, there was a flicker of insight and I realized this was just social talk. Anybody who was seeing me after a gap of two years—unshaven, emaciated, hollow faced—would say, 'You do not look well. Is something wrong?'

Shamsie did not notice my distraction. She had enough going on in her own head. For one, they had no place to live.

'Is it okay if we stay here for a day? Tomorrow, we will go to the *dera* and stay there until we find a proper place. Sidhu has got us a letter of reference, for jobs, and housing too.'

Shamsie went upstairs to cook lunch and I had Bheem for company, who told me about Maharashtra politics around the issue of dance bars.

Later, the sun came out, the fog melted away and even my gloom became several shades lighter. By the time Shamsie announced lunch, I was back among the living. The rooms had been tidied up. Shamsie had taken a bath, and her hair was open. She was wearing a towel robe of mine, which I had not seen for years, and a pair of old flip-flops that I did not know still existed. The bed was freshly made with a clean bedspread. The clothes in the cupboard were on hangers, the gas stove was gleaming, and the jars and bottles arranged. For a moment again, I had this feeling of my blessed privacy being invaded. But when I saw the dress which she must have been wearing during travel and a wet towel on the clothesline on the terrace, the house felt like home. I had not had such a feeling since my divorce.

'We left in a hurry, could not get anything for you,' Shamsie said, while frying *tadka* for the daal. 'And I just found out you do not drink.' She pointed at her glass on the kitchen shelf and then to the bottle of Peter Scot she had brought me all those many years ago. 'I threw away the Feni. It was all fungus.'

I asked Bheem for a song in the evening. We went out to the terrace. The fog was back, dark, and swirling, like a living thing. We could not see even each other. Bheem sang, his voice sad and tender, permeating the fog and floating over the river.

> *Take away the earth*
> *Take away the word*
> *Take away the meaning too*
> *Take away the ancient*
> *Take away the sun*
> *Just leave me the night*
> *It's in the night that Laila*
> *Comes out of Majnu's side*
> *She'll come yet*
> *For the earth's still wet*
> *And the footprints fresh.*

Before leaving, the next morning, Shamsie asked what I knew about Dera Garibparvar. I told her the bits and pieces I had heard from my patients, Jeet, and from newspapers over the years.

When I came up after seeing them off, there was a thank you note stuck on the fridge. It also said that she was taking the leftover whisky so that it did not go waste.

Eighteen

Dera Garibparvar was at least one hundred years old, probably older. Spread across 700 acres of undulating land along the northern bank of Beas before the river merged into the Satluj, it was the crown jewel among a score of *deras* dotting the landscape, where people, disillusioned with the bureaucracy of Hinduism and Sikhism, sought spiritual solace.

The *dera* had started as a Sufi *mazaar* on a small piece of rocky land on the riverbank. Folklore has it that one morning, about a hundred years back, a large mound of freshly dug earth was found by three fishermen, two of whom were Muslim and one Hindu of the Chamar caste. The mound of moist earth had atop it a *sarkanda* stick with a dirty piece of red cloth tied to it. More fishermen had collected, and someone mentioned that the man who used to sing Sufi songs and collect alms in the villages had not been seen for days, which was rather unusual, because nobody remembered when he had last gone missing for so long. A passer-by came forward and said that he had, the previous night, seen a grave being dug at the same spot by a bearded man in black robes with a green halo around his head. It seemed an angel had descended to mark Roda Darvesh's grave.

The young Sufi singer was hairless. He had no hair on his head and face, and had no eyebrows or eyelashes. That was the reason he was called Roda Darvesh, the hairless seer. Roda Darvesh had a large tin can tied to his waist with a long jute string. The sound produced by the can bumping against the ground announced his arrival as he entered a lane. He would then sit under a tree or on the doorsteps of a house and sing songs with words like Allah, Maula, Murshid, and Guru. People did not understand the meaning completely, but he had a soulful voice and women pampered him. They would come and put wheat, rice, jaggery, or a paisa or two in the cloth bag, which lay open next to him. They looked with awe at the pale hairless man, as if he was a miracle sent by God himself and prayed silently with folded hands for a wish to be fulfilled. The *darvesh* would keep muttering as if conversing with himself and never replied. However, if he did not get up and leave right away, it was presumed that the wish would be considered. After a minute or an hour, whenever he so fancied, Roda Darvesh would abruptly get up, gather his bag, and walk away with the can trailing behind him.

As news of the discovery of a fresh burial place spread, tales of Roda Darvesh's blessings and miracles multiplied.

It seemed that several childless couples, many dying patients, and some invalid children had been the beneficiaries.

A management trust of sorts was constituted on the spot, with the three original discoverers of the grave as the founding members. A hundred rupees were collected from the nearby villages, and a room of bricks and clay built in a couple of days. The clay came from the riverside and bricks were the ones discarded as deformed at a kiln two miles upstream. A proper cemented grave was built around the mound of clay and a rather large flag of a red triangular cloth with shiny green margins fixed at the top of the room.

Childless couples, hypochondriac men, unhappy daughters-in-law, suspicious wives, and the jobless— Muslims, Hindus, Sikhs, and a smattering of freshly converted Christians too—started flocking to Roda Darvesh's *mazaar* since the *darvesh* could no longer come to them. Some devotees must have had their prayers answered, because the trickle soon became a flow. All those who came left a coin or two, flowers, and some rice or wheat. A trust member's son, Aslam, who did not do anything except smoke weed, which grew wild along the riverbed, was asked to live there to collect offerings and manage the crowds. The fact that Aslam would not only hear voices and see visions when intoxicated, but also talked back to them animatedly, helped a lot. He even danced with the apparitions he saw and people in the crowd would chant and sway in harmony with him. This lent an even stronger mystical aura to the place.

The people who came from distant villages could not have gone back the same day. So, an inn and a kitchen were constructed. A boundary wall and gate were erected around the area, which expanded manifold over successive generations. Hand pumps were dug, which was the easiest part, since water was just 10 feet below the ground, the river being so close. The *mazaar* got electricity, even before many houses in the towns nearby, because the area tehsildar's wife had delivered not one but two sons, six years after their marriage, by praying just once at the *mazaar*.

When the country split into two in 1947, it was Aslam's grandson, Murshid, who held the seat of the now prosperous *mazaar*. The trust had two more members, Bilal Ahmed and Gopal Chamar, whose ancestors, along with Aslam's father, were the ones who had first discovered the mound of earth with the piece of red cloth fluttering atop it.

Murshid was a demi-god for the Muslims, Sikhs, and Hindus of the area, which was now destined to be part of India. The idea of giving up the divine seat, and the cash and gold that came along with it, just to go to the new Muslim country did not even cross Murshid's mind. Abandoning his hold over hundreds of thousands of followers to go to Pakistan, where he had nothing at all and where nobody knew him, seemed ridiculous, even after the killings and the exodus of Muslims began. Not even after Bilal, the only other Muslim trustee had taken advantage of an Army truck going to the border 50 miles away. Neither Murshid nor Bilal knew that the army truck had been arranged by Gopal Chamar. Within a span of two weeks, the *dera* was full of terrified Muslim families on their way to Pakistan with their trunks, canisters, and clothes tied in bed sheets in the hope that the

Sikh and Hindu marauders would leave alone an exalted place of worship. Hindus and Sikhs living in nearby villagers were equally devout followers of the *dera,* they argued in desperation. For some time, the oasis of peace remained just that. A sanctuary surrounded by a sea of mayhem, in which thousands travelling towards the freshly drawn border had been looted and killed, caravans of boats had been sunk in the river, and trains carrying just dead bodies had reached their destination.

The uneasy calm at the *dera* lasted for 10 days. On the eleventh, a band of Sikh and Hindu men, supposedly outsiders, which just meant nobody recognized them, scaled the gate and all hell broke loose. They shot at and stabbed to death all the Muslim men, women, and children taking shelter there. The dead included the *dera* head, Murshid Hussain, and his family. While belongings of the dead Muslims were fair game, no women were taken away alive and nothing belonging to the *dera* was touched, not the money, nor the gold, and the buildings were left standing and unscathed.

The narrators of the Partition days tell endless stories about how Hindus and Sikhs protected Muslim families on this side of the border, while Muslims did the same on the other side. While these stories are true, there are countless others of killings and massacres like the one Gopal had orchestrated. Butcheries occurred for the sake of property or gold, to eliminate a business rival or just as an act of revenge for an old grouse, striking when the iron was hot. These were cold-blooded murders disguised as Partition killings and are less frequently written about. Probably, because it was difficult to ascertain motives in the middle of a conflagration which went on for weeks and which had consumed a million people by the time it was doused. And, because there is nothing remarkable about human greed to write about.

After a decent interval of five days, a solemn meeting was held at the *dera* to mourn the dead. At the end of the meeting, the gathering nominated the only surviving member of the trust, Gopal Chamar, as the *dera* head. The nomination was not smooth. The Jats, which formed a vociferous force among the congregation even if their numbers were smaller, tried to block Gopal from taking over the powerful *dera*. However, Gopal was one of the only two trust members alive and the other having fled to Pakistan was not available.

Gopal knew exactly what needed to be done in the weeks and months that followed the Partition. Two-thirds of the *dera* followers had been Muslims. All of them had either been killed or had gone to Pakistan. And what is a *dera* without followers? In a neat operation planned to replace the *dera's* congregation, Gopal threw open the doors to the rush of Hindu and Sikh refugees pouring unendingly over the border. The space and buildings were there and so was money. Rows of tents were pitched to make more room. Doctors and nurses were available as volunteers from the towns nearby. Many of the people who came in were professionals and skilled workers, happy to be alive and keen to help. There were doctors, compounders, nurses, carpenters, shopkeepers, accountants, plumbers, cooks, and gardeners among the refugees taking shelter in the *dera*. There were all categories of workers, except chamars and scavengers, who had not migrated since they had nothing to lose by staying back except the lowest rung of the ladder in the Hindu religion. They simply shifted to the lowest rung of the ladder of Islam and stayed back.

The ones who had come were eager to use their craft in running the *dera*. They had to stay there for some time anyway, as they waited for the rest of their families to join them, searched for jobs, and filed property claims in government offices in lieu of the homes they had left behind.

The *dera* found mention in international newspapers as a place of succour and selfless service, which helped thousands of bodies and souls to heal. No doubt, all of that did happen. In as much as human motives are complex and intentions tangled, what was also achieved by Gopal at the end of six months was a slick substitution of his congregation by even more devout followers who repaid their debt by several times more, over the decades and generations to come.

Most of the new parishioners belonged to a religion not simply different from the previous one, but also carried deep wounds received at the hands of Muslims. Since the religion of the priest too had changed, it helped. Gopal came from a family of leather workers, but had never done any skinning or tanning himself. He was a trader in cattle hides. He gave up this profession and became a full-time godman. Gopal already had long hair, which he left open. He also started putting three lines of vermilion across his forehead and now called himself Guru Gopal Ram, which was a clever amalgamation of names of two Hindu gods. Over his pale white kurta-pyjama, he now wore long saffron robes with wooden sandals and several rows of rudraksh beads around his neck and wrist, completing his transformation. It was difficult to walk in wooden sandals, but Gopal Ram knew he did not have to go anywhere for the rest of his life and that the world would come to him instead. And it did.

The next change was to move the grave of Roda Darvesh out of the sanctum sanctorum. Gopal Ram's first thought was to do away with the *mazaar* completely, but he was a good judge of his new flock. He knew that although almost all of his new followers were Hindus and Sikhs, they had a fascination for Muslim peers and dargahs, and it would be a good strategy to celebrate the one they already had in-house. He decided to keep the *mazaar*, but relocate it to another part of the grounds. His heart was set on reserving the central sanctum all for himself, with him sitting on a throne, resplendent in his robes, blessing the gathering, and keeping a watchful eye on the offerings.

The shift necessitated the unpleasant task of digging up the *mazaar* and transferring the interred remains of Roda Darvesh to a fresh grave at a place in the open. This was a task for the night. All the workers and devotees who lived there permanently had a steadfast loyalty to Gopal Ram. However, digging up the grave of a saint, even when respectfully following the protocol, was a sensitive matter. Also, Muslim *peers*, particularly the dead ones, were rumoured to have a punitive side.

The only person who would do the digging without question was Sheikh Abbasi. Sheikh Abbasi never questioned anything concerning the *dera*. He was a *bhishti*, whose job was to go around the grounds and pour water into the cupped palms of thirsty devotees from the goatskin bag called *mashq* that he carried on his back. His father and grandfather had done the same at the *dera* and he was the lone Muslim left now. Both his parents died when he was a child and he had been brought up in the *dera*; the only bond he felt was with his *peer* Roda Darvesh. On the day of the massacre, he had gone to the city to get the torn spout of his *mashq* stitched. On coming back, he had declared that he would not leave the side of his *peer* as long as he lived, no matter what happened.

Guru Gopal Ram chose Sheikh Abbasi, and only him, for the task. Marble slabs, bricks, cement, and masonry tools were ready at the freshly dug-up site outside in the open, a hundred yards away from the sanctum. Things were explained and left to the Bhishti, who seemed overwhelmed by the enormity of the task entrusted to him. Gopal Ram did not think his own presence was necessary and he went off to sleep at his usual time. He woke up at midnight with a lantern shining in his eyes, behind which was the blanched face of Sheikh Abbasi, who seemed to have seen a ghost. The Bhishti was laughing, crying, blabbering, and pulling at Gopal Ram's hand like a child. At the best of times, he was a simpleton, content to do his job, and pray several times a day at the *mazaar* of the only god he knew. Gopal Ram followed him to the shrine. The vast room was now heaps of bricks, marble tiles, and loose earth. When he lowered the lantern into the pit in the middle of the room, the sight shook Gopal Ram too. At the bottom of the pit lay what were unmistakably the skeletal remains of an average sized dog. Remnants of a leather collar with a buckle of dark rust completed the picture.

Gopal Ram stepped away from the heap of loose earth and bolted the heavy door shut, as it was done every night at the time of counting the day's offerings. He was a quick-thinking man and pieced together what must have happened. The three fishermen who had found the fresh burial place with a piece of red cloth fluttering atop had presumed it was the missing *darvesh* under that mound of earth, because nobody else had gone missing. The man who had said that he had seen an angel digging a grave at night must have been high on weed. The discoverers of the burial mound could not have imagined that a hunter of *nilgais*, with which the forest along the river was thickly populated, could have lost his dog to an illness or snakebite. The hunter did what any dog lover would have done. He had buried the dog there and since it had been his favourite dog, put a flag on the spot as a sign of his affection.

The Bhishti sat on his haunches with his head in his arms, whimpering loudly and feeling devastated. It was shocking for Gopal Ram too, but not for such existential reasons. Generations of men and women from hundreds of miles around had not only prayed at that *mazaar*, but also had had their prayers answered. Many invalids who had been carried there went back home walking, childless women had conceived within a month, and unfaithful husbands had turned virtuous. The shops outside the *dera* sold illustrated booklets of the legend of Roda Darvesh, with old pictures of the shrine and a hairless youth. These low quality images could be easily explained; cameras were not common at the time and sketches of the *darvesh* were drawn from memory. But who could explain away that the one buried and revered, in whose name millions of rupees worth of gold, cash, and grains had been given as offerings over the decades, was not even a man, but a dog! Gopal Ram knew one thing for sure. If this came out, he would be lynched by the mobs who would not believe that neither he nor any of his ancestors knew. Even if they were to believe him, his income would surely come to an abrupt halt.

Looking at Sheikh Abbasi moaning and writhing on the floor like a stricken animal, Gopal Ram knew that the Bhishti would not be able to keep this secret to himself. He was too simple for that. By the next morning, everyone would know that the congregation and their ancestors had been victims of a cruel fraud. Nobody would remember the massive relief work done by him for the thousands of people ravaged by the Partition of India.

When the *dera* workers woke up in the morning, Roda Darvesh had a gleaming new resting place in the open, much bigger than before. It was covered with white marble tiles brought from Makrana in Rajasthan. The new *mazaar* had steps on its four sides, on which red roses from the *dera* garden and yellow water lilies from the river lay scattered. Lighted incense sticks, stuck in tiny brass stands on the flat of the grave, infused the morning air with sacred fragrance.

The previous night, Gopal Ram had hated his ancestors for being fools. He was a man who liked precision and predictability. So, the previous night, he had rectified a-century-old wrong and ensured for his followers and his own future generations that the remains buried under the marble came not just from the right species, but also from the right religion.

On the next Puranmasi, the full moon night, Guru Gopal Ram ensconced himself on a throne in the sanctum and rechristened himself Mahaprabhu, the great god.

For a few days, the *dera* residents talked about how Sheikh Abbasi was so upset after shifting the resting place of the *darvesh* that he had quietly left for Pakistan, the same night.

Nobody wondered why a *bhishti* would leave behind something as inseparable from him as his goatskin *mashq.*

Nineteen

Bheem and Shamsie made their way to Dera Garibparvar travelling by a long-distance bus going to Amritsar that dropped them at the ornate gates adorned with pillars, security pickets, metal detectors, and sniffer dogs.

The *dera* was now several times bigger than it was after the Partition. It was a proper township with 15 sectors, two inns, a hospital, water works, four schools, two colleges with hostels, a supermarket, an electric crematorium, and an airstrip, all of which were owned and administered by the *dera*. Then there was an electricity sub-station, a railway station, and a post office owned and run by the government, but staffed by persons nominated by the *dera*. The hangar at the airstrip housed a nine-seater executive jet, donated by the New Jersey chapter of the Mahaprabhu's followers. There was also a helipad that remained busy during elections, one or the other of which was always underway. Between the parliamentary elections, state assembly elections, local body elections, or some bye-election in the interim, there was never a dull moment. During these times, politicians came in droves from all over the country, including Delhi, to ask for blessings and, of course, votes. The railway station catered only to *dera* residents and the visitors to the *dera* but all trains, even the superfast ones, stopped there.

The residential sectors had mid- to large-sized houses with lawns, and some even had swimming pools. In many of the larger houses lived retired bureaucrats and police officers. Having done justice to their life in this birth, they were now trying to better their spirituality ratings for use in the next, through prayer, meditation, and helping out in smooth running of the *dera* administration.

The oldest parts of the *dera*, including the public prayer arena, the semi-private meditation hall, the private blessing room, and Mahaprabhu's sprawling residence behind several layers of security, were all in the rear part of the township. Roda Darvesh's *mazaar* was still popular, although it was no longer the main attraction. It had been walled off and had a separate entrance, which opened to the public only on Thursdays when people would come for prayers and *qawwalis* in praise of Roda Darvesh. The blessings that devotees wished for had remained monotonously the same over the last hundred years. There were still the invalids, childless couples, jobless youths, and wives trying to mend wayward husbands. The offerings at the *mazaar* had increased several folds, but were modest for the times. A deputy from the *dera*, who appeared to be Muslim from the skullcap and salwar he wore on Thursdays, would be in attendance, handing over amulets to be worn, armbands to be tied, and ashes to be placed under pillows.

The main Garibparvar Dera, which literally meant 'nurturer of the poor', had also transformed. The devotees came from all over the country and had travelled long distances by air, trains, and sleek chauffeur-driven cars. Their wishes were pretty much the same as at the *mazaar*. There were young daughters not finding a suitable match, boys who refused to do a day's work, and of course, the childless couples. These devotees came with families and stayed at the inns, which could rival any five-star hotel with their spas, gyms, and swimming pools. The waiting list for the Mahaprabhu's darshan was about a week. According to a strict egalitarian principle, no prior appointments were given. Mahaprabhu blessed people on a first come, first served basis. Meanwhile, families spent quality time swimming, exercising, meditating, and watching religious discourses by the Mahaprabhu on the devotional channel owned by the *dera* that was telecast all over the country. The international channel adjusted for local timings of other countries and even for daylight saving time changes twice a year. The best part was that no bill was presented to the devotees at the end of their stay since the inns were free. They were, however, encouraged to give donations several times more than what the bills would have been. For this, they were given proper receipts which typically stated, 'Received a sum of rupees five lakh only on account of donation from Soul Narendra Nath Bhatia'. All anointed followers of the *dera* were called Souls. Soul Bhatia would pass the receipt to his accountant upon his return, for a tax rebate. The *dera*, of course, did the same as donations were not taxable, whereas income from the inns would have been. The cash and gold offerings presented directly to the Mahaprabhu, in the private blessing chamber during the darshan, were widely known to be more substantial. But these were not a matter of public record. A retired commissioner of income tax who was a Soul too, lived in one of the larger houses and advised the *dera* accountants on such matters.

The incumbent Mahaprabhu was the eldest son of Gopal Chamar, the first Hindu head. Since the *dera* had been headed by lower caste men now for two generations, it held a special appeal for Dalits. The Mahaprabhu did not make any effort to either dispel that impression or encourage it. When specifically asked, he insisted that since all Souls were equal children of one God, who was he to tell one from the other. However, there was a clear difference in the relationship the two distinct congregations had with the *dera*.

For Dalits, it was a place that validated their being human. Unlike temples and gurudwaras, there was no part of the *dera* where their caste would be even asked, including in the prayer and meditation halls. For the first time, there was a space—a sprawling, clean, prosperous world-famous space—where they were not only welcome and accepted as equal, but which also gave them unconditional comradeship and a sense of belonging that their ancestors had craved for centuries. There were hospitals for the sick and schools with qualified teachers for the children. Everything was free. They even got well-paying jobs with clean uniforms, free meals, and retirement benefits. Despite all his talk of equality, the Mahaprabhu trusted only Dalit Souls for the *dera*'s and his own personal security.

In addition to the donations, money earned through the sale of memorabilia, like pendants with the Mahaprabhu's glowing face on them, T-shirts ('Proud to be a Soul', 'I am a cool Soul', and 'Mahaprabhu rocks'), CDs and DVDs of the Mahaprabhu's sermons, as also the income from the TV channel and the sound and light show was more than enough to run the *dera* and its facilities. Ministers from both the state and central governments visited, even when there were no elections, and donated cheques for large amounts from government funds under different headings, such as Sports Promotion (for the new stadium), Female Education (for the new girls' college), and Youth Welfare (for the new gym with the latest equipment). This was quite sufficient for the *dera*'s expansion.

The *dera*'s big money came from solving the problems of visitors in business suits, mostly men and the occasional women, who came by the morning train and left in the afternoon by the same train on its return journey. Each of them fixed an appointment, days in advance. They were driven from the railway station to the office block, a two-storied building equipped with computers, secretaries, a pantry, and a boardroom. The visitors did not meet Mahaprabhu. They did not need to, nor were they particularly keen to. They met instead Soul Ramola, an MBA from a highly sought-after business school.

She listened to the visitors who were senior managers from business houses all over the country. Ramola was impeccably dressed in a formal wear, complete with a tie. The only hint that she was a functionary of a holy place was the discrete saffron dot on her forehead. Ramola quickly grasped the regulatory bottlenecks that visitors' businesses had run into or intricacies of the upcoming government contracts they were eyeing. She was able to make quick decisions, since it all depended on the specific ministers involved and the *dera*'s relationship with them. The idea was not to pressurize the ministers and rob them of their rightful due, but to strike reasonable deals with them.

Followers of the Garibparvar Dera were concentrated in North India, but were spread all over the country in significant numbers. Twenty million of them were eligible voters. Of course, the Mahaprabhu was not interested in politics and the *dera* spokespersons had to issue repeated press statements during elections that the *dera* followers must vote according to the dictates of their own conscience. However, after each election result, dark suited psephologists on TV would conclude that the Souls had voted en bloc and swayed the result. That was the only reason the *dera* had a helipad. So that aspiring kings could come and pay homage to the kingmaker.

Soul Ramola did not make any promises, but, somehow, a good number of tasks that had seemed impossible ended up being done and contracts granted at a reasonable cost. Almost simultaneously, large 'donations' got made to the Dera Garibparvar's and Mahaprabhu's bank accounts overseas.

***

The set of tall gates at the entrance of the *dera* were heavily fortified. There were snipers in pillboxes at the top of the turrets. One had to pass through two metal gates, one after the other, that were never open at the same time. Between the two gates, on both sides of the road, were men armed with automatic rifles, whose olive helmets were visible behind columns of sandbags. Armed guards had always been there the old timers recalled, but the automatic rifles, not necessarily legal, came later after the start of the Naxalite militancy that preceded the Khalistani one. Leftist revolutionaries disliked the *dera*, because they did not like religion in general and the concentration of wealth and power in particular. The right religious extremists, the Boys too despised all *dera*s, but because of a different reason. The followers of each *dera* worshipped a living human being and that is an anathema in Sikhism. Yet, the leaders of the movement did not want to alienate Dalits who formed one-third of the people of the state and the highest concentration of Dalits in the country, particularly when some Dalit Sikhs were militants too.

Bheem and Shamsie handed over their reference letter from the MLA who had been elected on a seat reserved for Dalits. The letter had been procured for them by Sidhu.

There was an office attached to the gates from where the security officer faxed the letter to somebody senior inside. Five minutes later, the reply scrolled out of the machine with instructions. The security officer, a retired army captain in uniform, screened Bheem with a metal detector and a young woman in khaki trousers and a hip holster patted down Shamsie. Their bags were scanned and the Peter Scot whisky bottle taken out. Along with the Wills Navy Cut packet from Shamsie's pocket, it was put in a plastic bag, which was sealed and numbered. Shamsie was given a token in lieu of those. The woman, whose name plate read Soul Mala, smiled at her sweetly and said in a sincere voice, 'The air here is so calming that you will not need it. If you want it back, when you leave the *dera* you can pick it up, but most people do not. And then, we do not know what to do with these.' With that, she opened with a flourish the door of a long cupboard lining the wall with rows of bottles ranging from Scotch whisky to country hooch and several packets of what looked like opium husk, cigarettes, biris, and tobacco pouches.

'In fact, many people do not even leave the *dera* once they have been here for some days. You are welcome to Dera Garibparvar, Madam Gurshamsheer and Bheem Sir.'

Twenty

I would wake up groggy from the effect of sleeping pills. The day was a viscous stream that had somehow to be crossed. There were no thoughts, not even bad ones. There was just this blankness. I had not gone to see Dr Mustafa for three months and indulged in an orgy of self-medication with random drugs in senseless combinations. I would write prescriptions for fake patients and Jeet would buy those for me. At least I slept, but it was a knocked-out sleep, the sort that left my mind unrested. There were days when walking into the river seemed like the best idea ever. For its part, the edge of the water had been creeping towards my house as if it were a message. Jeet said it was not unusual for this part of the year. I did not feel like seeing patients at all. In fact, I hated them for reminding me how contented I used to be around them and now was not. I imagined I had made mistakes, even when I had not. One particularly dusty morning, I ran bare feet after a couple after my flip-flops broke, while scrambling out of my chair. I thought I had written some horribly wrong injection for their child. They had gone ahead walking and it took me a while to catch up.

They were startled when they saw me bare-feet and panting, my stethoscope still hanging around my neck. I snatched the prescription from the father's hand, took a quick look, and gave it back, sheepishly saying that I just wanted to check the dose. I came back and put up a cardboard sign at the gate, which read that the clinic would remain closed 'till further notice' because I had to go away due to a bereavement in the family. Death was the only thing patients respected. If I had written I was ill, they would have walked up to ask how I was feeling. Jeet, of course, knew I had no family.

I was left alone, but after seeing the board, either the terrorists or the policemen started using the ground floor of my house, at night, as a resting or meeting spot or for laying an ambush.

I do not think they knew I was sleeping upstairs all along. Otherwise, they would have brought me down to treat their injuries, because some mornings I saw blood on the floor and blood stains on the doorknob. More than that it was the unflushed toilets and the stink that left me disturbed. After some days, the shit of the holy warriors, of the police, or of both, not that you could tell, made me take the board down. I got the place cleaned up by the sweepers brought by Jeet, using garden hoses. When I came down in the afternoon, they showed me empty bottles of country liquor, pouches of snacks, four used cartridges, and some condom wrappers.

'Is this the police or the terrorists?' I asked Jeet.

'There was a time when one could tell,' he said wistfully.

Three days later, I was kidnapped by the terrorists for providing my house to the police to ambush their 'freedom fighters'.

I was still in my nightclothes trying to untangle the bougainvillea vine from the rose bush in my garden that overlooked the river, not because I felt like it, but because Dr Mustafa had recommended it at one time as part of my treatment. That advice had at that time caused me a lot of dismay, because I knew some doctors recommended gardening and long walks only when they had reached a dead end.

'No, it is not like that,' he had seen my expression crumble. 'If you tend to life, your mind is nurtured too. If you create order out of disorder, your thoughts get organized too.' So, in untangling that tenacious vine with purple flowers from the rose bush, I was hoping for a mirror change in my mind. But before my mind could reap the fruits of my labour, I was lifted off my feet by a tall Sikh and, dangling between his arm and waist, was carried outside and thrown in the back seat of an Ambassador car with dark windowpanes, which in fact were banned those days. I was going to remind him of that, but another pair of hands gagged and blindfolded me with what appeared to be a georgette cloth from the crinkly feel. My hands were tied with a plastic twine, which cut sharply into the wrists. The driver knew his way and no directions were given. The road became increasingly bumpy over the next two hours and the sound of traffic infrequent. There was a loo break and after the driver and my escorts had been, it was my turn. My hands were untied, blindfold loosened to hang around my neck, and I was turned around to face a direction, which I initially presumed to be fields, but the earth under my feet felt too yielding and all that I saw was a long stretch of mud and slush in every direction.

It was mid-morning and, since nobody stopped the car with darkened panes, I was convinced it was the police that had abducted me. The last stretch of the journey was a walk in deep mud. The chappals I was wearing had slipped off when I was hoisted. I heard the car trunk opening and closing. I was made to sit on the ground and could feel my feet being wrapped in plastic carry bags, which were then tied around my shins with tight rubber bands. My hands were untied again so that I could balance myself while walking in the marsh. It took us half an hour squelching through the swamp. The blindfolds and gag were removed at the other end. Both my kidnappers were tall young Sikhs with athletic builds, open beards, and intense eyes.

It was an old brick structure, most of which had crumbled over the decades. I thought I knew where I was. Back in the time of the Mughals, this was where the road from Delhi to Lahore passed. In those days, there were inns along the way for travellers and their horses to rest at night. This seemed to be one of those ruins. The Liberation Army had appropriated the place and dug bunkers inside. I was asked to remove the plastic bags from my feet and along with my escorts.I walked down a long flight of stairs, which had no handrail.

The basement was a different world altogether. There were corridors like burrows in all directions, intersecting like a complex maze with doors at random intervals. The rough plastered walls, which exposed thin and rough bricks wherever the plaster had worn off, were so damp that they dripped. There was water on the floor, but the doors were new and of seasoned wood meant to last. The plaster seemed to have been at least five years old. I recalled Jeet telling me what his father had told him. That most cycles of terrorism played out for 10 years, before burning out. If they did not, there would be another 10 years' cycle. We had been in the second cycle for more than a year. Most Punjabis by then, including the terrorists, I suppose, were trying to guess how and when it would end, as everybody, probably including them, wanted it to. Excitement has its own inbuilt ennui.

Several twists and turns after walking bare feet on the cold, wet floor, I was shoved through a door. It was somebody's bedroom, a spartan 10x10, with a camp cot and two metal chairs. And an attached loo. I should have been worried for my life, but my mind was preoccupied with figuring out how the toilet worked against gravity in this basement. Maybe, I was too scared. Maybe, I did not care what would happen next. There must be generators and pressure motors for the plumbing, I concluded, before the door opened and a tall man, probably in his late 50s, who had to bend to enter, said, 'I somehow knew it would be you.'

The man was remarkably familiar. He certainly knew me. He was wearing an olive turban and shiny black shoes, had pockmarked skin and a military bearing, and smiled like a child who has found a lost toy.

'General Dhillon,' he introduced himself. 'You gave me your blood pressure medicines three years back. I sort of owed you one.'

I remembered the history teacher in a police lockup, beaten to pulp with sky high blood pressure. The history teacher who, as it turned out, was also an ex-army officer. A general, in fact, and a strategy expert of the liberation force.

'When I was told that a Hindu doctor in that area had given his house to police snipers and thus had to be eliminated, I said I wanted to see him first.'

I told General Dhillon how the ground floor of my house was used by anyone during those days without my knowledge or consent, and that I was too sick to care. I also told him about the empty booze bottles and condom wrappers.

'Definitely not ours,' his face was clouded with anger.

I told him that in my milkman's opinion, one could not tell these days.

'If that is what people think of us, it is bad news.'

I told him about the used cartridges, and how the packets had Urdu writing on them.

'And the condoms?'

'Same. Urdu.'

'So, your milkman may have been right. But our boys drinking and copulating on duty! Even the Indian Army does not do that.'

'The liquor bottles did not have Urdu markings,' I reassured him, 'and there were three police ID cards.'

'Those, too, are ours. Our boys use them all the time. So, it seems our fighters were using your house to shoot at our fighters. Might as well go to Australia and live with my daughter.'

I was asked to put the plastic wrappers back on my feet and was escorted across the marsh to the Ambassador car and dropped back at my house around lunchtime.

The next morning, in the tiny patch that was my garden, I again started attempting to put my internal world in order by untangling the bougainvillea vine from the rose bush and while my mind was even showing some early signs by becoming less turbulent, it was the external world that was rocked again. I was lifted away this time by a tall policeman in uniform and thrown into the back of another Ambassador car with dark panes and taken to the police station across the pontoon bridge. This was the same place with the water-logged ground floor where I had, three years earlier, answered questions about my stolen car and agreed, under duress, with Maai-baap that 'Zahid sharaab peene de' was written by Ghalib, although it was not. I was put in a cold and damp cell. Nobody came for me for two days, except for a 10-year boy with buns in a basket and dirty tea glasses in a wire frame. I hardly slept since I did not have my medicines and the withdrawal caused retching. When I asked a policeman for permission to call Jeet so he could bring my medicines, I was told it was a police lock up and not my in-laws' house.

On the third or fourth or fifth day, I was not sure which, I was pulled out of the cell, weak and limp. Held by my arms with feet dragging along the unhewn floor, I was brought to the same sprawling office with two doors missing and fungus growing on its damp walls. This was where I had once been interrogated by Maai-baap about my missing car that was later found to be involved in the bloody massacre at the police station. I could hardly stand up, but, surprisingly, in my head, I did not feel quite so bad. In fact, I quipped with the policemen supporting me if the feathers on their turbans were real or plastic. I also made a mental note to ask Dr Mustafa to publish a paper on 'Arrest as a non-pharmacological treatment of resistant depression'. In my now agile mind, I even anticipated his rejoinder, 'Nothing to do with arrest. It is just sleep deprivation. Everybody already knows it works. Why bother?'

'Fine. You just forgot to tell me that. I could as well have tried it at home rather than gardening, which led to me being kidnapped. Twice!'—I would have complained.

I was deposited either on the same tall wooden stool as the last time, or one very similar.

Maai-baap entered from the door connecting the office to a room at the rear. He was wearing a uniform with an Ashoka emblem and two stars on the epaulettes and colourful feathers in his turban. The missing golf cap meant it was not a Sunday, the only indication of the weekly calendar my mind had sensed so far. The turban made him look taller, but when he sat in that low chair, he reminded me of a hawk looking up at his prey.

'Why have I been arrested?' I wanted to know.

'You have not been arrested,' he stared back blankly.

'Then why am I here?'

'You are not here. You are mistaken.' He looked straight into my eyes with the hurt expression of an honest man being blamed.

'Then where am I if not here?' I asked.

'With due respect, it is not my job to keep track of your locations. All I know is that you are not here, although you seem to think you are. It seems to be an honest difference of opinion.'

'I have been here the last three or four or five days, lying folded in cell number 6.' He looked up and down a register lying on the table and said, 'Cell number 6 has been empty for six months.'

'Your men picked me up from my house when I was tending to my plants.'

'My men follow the rules and would never pick up an innocent man. They are working in difficult circumstances. Their job is to arrest terrorists. Are you one?'

'No, I am a doctor.'

'You can be both. Two in one. Like Dr Jekyll and Mr Hyde. Doctor during the day and a friend of the terrorists at night. You even have a record. Three years ago, you lent your car to terrorists to carry out an attack on a police station in which six policemen were killed and a terror master mind escaped. I interrogated you myself. In this very room.'

'But you let me go because you verified and found that my car had actually been stolen.'

'And this time, I should let you go, because your house had *actually* been stolen and used by terrorists? Eh? You think we are assholes?'

I wanted to talk to him about this bizarre anal fixation of his, but I was carried back and deposited in cell number 6, which continued to be empty. Pending transfer to the Gym via the Gaayab Road whenever a vacancy occurred there, I was told.

I continued to not sleep and became increasingly euphoric, which of course meant that the abrupt stoppage of medication after continuous use for eight years and the lack of sleep had unhinged my brain even more. I would call the passing policemen and ask them to sing a song for me, 'Any song will do. Even a sad one.' Another day, I asked them for a radio so I could listen to Binaca Geet Maala. Later, I stopped asking for the radio, because there was no need. I started hearing the voice of Ameen Sayani of Binaca Geet Mala from Radio Ceylon, which in fact had stopped airing it many years back. But I could clearly hear the jingles and the songs to which I gave my own rankings.

Two days or two weeks later, I was half dragged, and half carried by four men and was surprised to find Dr Mustafa and Jeet sitting in the office of Maai-baap who was wearing a golf cap, which meant it was a Sunday. Dr Mustafa had apparently given Maai-baap an affidavit that I was of unsound mind and not capable of planning my next meal, let alone hatching a conspiracy with terrorists. My old prescriptions and the hospital file had been attached to the statement. It further said that if the ground floor of my house had been used by terrorists, it must have been at night when I lay knocked out by drugs on the first floor.

I was released and taken to Dr Mustafa's ward in the medical college and admitted there for a month to rid me off the lilting melodies I had happily been listening to. Since I did not want treatment and created quite a ruckus, this was an involuntary admission signed by Jeet Singh, relation to the patient 'milkman', as my guardian.

Despite several changes in treatment and some injections imported from England, I kept hearing the voice of Ameen Sayani and even conversed with him about the ranking of songs. I spent one whole night sitting up in bed and arguing with him that 'Panna ki tamanna hai' deserved first place, rather than 'Mera jeevan kora kaagaz'. I was so loud that I kept other patients awake, who kept walking like zombies up and down the ward, since they had been sedated, but could not sleep due to my difference of opinion with Ameen Sayani and the loud arguments we both had although the patients could hear just my side. They cheered me along so I would win, and they could sleep.

Jeet told me afterwards that I was taken to a room in the OPD, thrice on alternate days, and given electric treatments under anaesthesia, which left me forgetful for an hour. When Sister Josephine came to my bed to pray for me, I, apparently, proposed to her. I told her I was willing to convert and be called Joseph Sylvester Pereira. Jeet said that she had agreed to leave the nunnery and marry me, but got angry over my choice of the name Pereira, because that meant I had Catholic leanings while she was a devout Protestant.

I initially thought the bit about Sister Josephine had been made up by Jeet to tease me. On the other hand, Jeet could not have thought of a name like Joseph Sylvester Pereira and, to tell the truth, Sister Josephine was stiffly officious with me on her follow-up visits.

At the end of a month, I had descended back to my morose self, without being suicidal in what Dr Mustafa described as a soft landing. I was discharged into the temporary care of my guardian, Jeet Singh, after he affixed the impression of his sole thumb on the form.

Twenty-one

There was an enormous parking lot next to the main gate of the *dera* and cars were not allowed beyond it. Electric buggies, which ran on rechargeable batteries, were the only way to move around, other than the bicycles used by the *dera* staff. This was a personal initiative by Mahaprabhu to inculcate environmental awareness among the souls and the visitors. The *dera* had received a grant of five crore rupees from the discretionary fund of the Minister of Environment for this project.

Shamsie and Bheem were sent to dormitory number 27, which had two more couples and their daughters who had been admitted to the residential school at the *dera*. The parents had come to leave the girls as the academic session was to start the next morning. There were many parents and kids in other dormitories. Many more would come in the morning.

Bheem had been quiet, quieter than usual since they had entered the *dera*. Shamsie prodded, 'What is wrong?'

'I do not like it here.' He was looking at his feet, which is what he did when he did not want a confrontation. They were having tea in the large canteen hall common to all the dormitories.

'What is there not to like already? We have not seen anything, nor met anybody. So far, what we have seen is a wide open, neat, and orderly place.' Shamsie looked at his face, trying to fathom what could be bothering him.

'It is too orderly. Like a military cantonment. I do not like that you will not be able to drink and smoke when you want to. Which was every day in Bombay.' Bheem continued to look down, his gaze now at the table, as he tried to scratch out its plywood pattern with his nails.

'You hardly drink. You do not smoke. It is my problem, not yours. Maybe, they are right. Maybe, the place does have something in its air, and one does not need to smoke or drink.'

Bheem stared at her in a stubborn manner, which was unusual, 'That is what I do not like about this place. It can change people. I do not want to change, and I do not want you to change. Not because of here.'

'You do not like religion, because you are a communist.' She regretted it the moment she said it. They had hardly ever discussed politics before and certainly never his.

'I am not a communist, because even that changes people and makes them automatons. Whenever the centre is too strong, everything else is weak. This place is even worse than communism, because while there the centre is an ideology, here it is a man, a man like you and me. You can argue about an ideology, but you cannot argue about a man who is supposed to be half God. Can you argue about Mahaprabhu?

You cannot. You are not even allowed to. I am fine as I am. I do not want to change, not because of this, he said, waving his arm in a sweeping gesture. 'I like myself and I like you. I do not want that to change either.' She wondered if there was hint of a threat there. Her hands stiffened, but the moment passed, and she tried to make light of his comment, 'So, you like me drinking and smoking?'

'I like you to not stop doing what you want to do. I want you to breathe freely. They will tame you here. Worst still, you will feel as if you are a free spirit, a "Soul". And that is not how I know you.'

Shamsie did not know what to make of Bheem's sudden sensitivity, so soon after entering the *dera* gates. She had never seen him like this. The idea of coming here seemed to be Sidhu's, but he was the one who had asked him to find out about the *dera*. Enthusiastically, in fact. So much so that she had suspected it was his idea to begin with. For the first time, she wondered whether she knew him at all. That thought was even more unsettling than the uncertainty about their future. It was probably the sudden change. Maybe, he needed more time. By the time evening came around, they had agreed to give it a week and see what the place had to offer. They had been instructed to not leave the *dera* for two days, as they could be summoned by Soul Ramola anytime. That happened on the third day, when Bheem had wandered away and Shamsie had to do some desperate running around before she found him sitting on the bank of an irrigation channel under a tree.

Ramola listened to Shamsie, in a placid unhurried manner, interjecting only with an occasional question for clarification, as Shamsie told her of her interest in dance and music. Even as Shamsie spoke, she wondered why a religious *dera* would be interested in a dancer. From what they had seen so far, with security men posted every few yards on the road, Bheem stood a better chance of finding a job at the *dera*.

They were told that the *dera* had, in fact, a thriving cultural division that had musicians and singers from around the country. What they had been looking for was a trained dancer. The *dera* encouraged performing arts and taught music and dance in their schools. The cultural troupe even travelled to other cities even abroad to hold public events for Indians and to spread the *dera*'s message of love and brotherhood. Bheem was to be hired as a security supervisor after vetting and a month of training. They would be given a two-room flat in one of the 'family blocks'.

That was when Bheem spoke.

'We are not a family.'

There was an awkward silence.

Ramola went through a file and took out the letter from the MLA who had recommended them.

'The letter says "couple". You are together, aren't you?'

Shamsie felt the moment slipping away. 'We have been together since we were children. We have always lived together, except when I was in the school hostel.' She looked at Bheem, waiting for him to confirm what she had said. Shamsie was baffled when he did not utter a word.

The *sadhvi's* tone was a shade magisterial when she spoke this time. 'The *dera* policies are progressive and liberal. However, living together as an arrangement is not permitted. One can either be a single like me,' she smiled in an attempt at levity, 'or married. We must be receptive towards the sensibilities of the larger *dera* community.' She followed this up by saying, 'Why don't you two get married? It can be arranged, even tomorrow, if you like. It will only take half an hour.' Since no one spoke, she added, 'I mean you have been together since childhood. Sooner or later, you will get married. Why not now?' Shamsie thought Sardarji had talked about it far more delicately.

'Because the only other option is for you to live in the working ladies' hostel and you in the men's,' she looked first at Shamsie and then at Bheem. 'You will still get the jobs. But we would prefer if you consider marriage sooner rather than later.'

Bheem got up, 'You have given us a lot to think about. We will need some time.'

'There is no hurry at all. You can live in the *dera* and take all the time you need. There is no pressure. Souls have been living here for years without working for the *dera*. But now that we know you are not married, you cannot be living in the family dormitory. Tomorrow morning, you will be assigned singles' accommodation.'

Bheem turned back from the door to ask, 'Is the title Soul compulsory?' He was looking at the nametag on the lapel of her black jacket.

'All records, ID documents, and name plates routinely carry that prefix and a number. These cannot be tailor-made for individual tastes. Even if one liked to be the odd person out.' She had a sharp tone unlike before.

'The woman is a fraud,' Bheem said under his breath the moment they were out of the room.

'I thought she was helpful and forthright. She did not waste any time. A bit tactless, but I liked her on the whole.'

'So, do we get married tomorrow?'

'You do not have to be sarcastic. I like the jobs they are offering, and we could live separately for some time.'

'Till when?'

'Till we are ready to get married.'

'She said sooner than later. You like the job a lot, don't you? Being on stage, all the dancing, fans, applause?'

'So what if I do?' She thought it was her legitimate turn to react. 'I stayed away from that for two years. I still can if there is something else to do, but there isn't. And if you have something up your sleeve, kindly offer it to me now.' She was the one looking unblinkingly at his face now.

Both were on unchartered ground here. The 'I' and 'You' had the feel of newly bought gadgets, an unfamiliar wariness with the thrill of the new.

'We have some money. We can live in the city and wait for something else to turn up.'

'Fine. We can wait for something to turn up, but until then, let us live and work here. Wasn't the whole idea of coming back to live in the *dera* because this place is safe?

Have things got any better outside? No. It is even more of a mayhem. And what is so poisonous in the air of this place that we should risk being slaughtered?'

'This place has already made us fight and pulled you away from me. You are suddenly fine with living separately after years of us living together. You are even fine with us getting married tomorrow, as if we are puppets. Because the place demands so. Of course, we would have gotten married eventually, but it would not have been forced upon us.'

They fought the whole night and slept at dawn. When Shamsie got up, the sun was high in the window and there was nobody else in the hall. There were six other unslept beds and next to her was Bheem's, which had been tidied up with the cover in place as was his habit. His backpack was gone. The watchman outside said that at 5, a man with a backpack had asked for a buggy to the gate.

***

The lawns on both sides of the road were immaculate, with the grass closely trimmed and the flowerbeds lined with rows of white painted bricks. Next to the road were rose bushes at least a hundred rows deep. Beyond the rose bushes, there was another hundred rows of deep violet Iris, and lastly, sunflowers that seemed to extend all the way to the horizon. The gardener Souls had made the best of the riverbank. There was a wooden bench in the middle of the rose garden with a narrow path leading to it. Bheem thought it possible that he was being hasty and, now that Shamsie was not around, decided to sit there to clear his head. He let the buggy go. The main gate was just a furlong away and he could see the turrets from where he sat. He knew if he walked out of that gate now, he would never come back. Knowing Shamsie as he did, if he went, it would be very unlike her to come looking for him.

What was wrong in staying here anyway? Shamsie would get to teach and dance. He would have a security supervisor's job. It would be better than what the two of them had in Bombay. And why shouldn't they get married? If he hated a *dera* sponsored marriage, they could live in different hostels till Sidhu organized their wedding in the city.

But that was not the reason Bheem was sitting on that bench instead of his bed next to Shamsie. It was the regimentation that he hated. He hated being labelled 'Soul number so and so'. In the three days he had been there, he had seen people coming in droves, prostrating at the gate before entering, hoping to have a glimpse of the Mahaprabhu and all the ostentation that went with it. His father had at least made himself happy by attending gate meetings and shouting slogans at the factory owners for the unpaid bonus and overtime. While the comrades had been exploited, what was being done to the devotees was evil, because it made them robots. The Souls were not left with their souls. He could not risk that even for a day. Not even for Shamsie.

He remembered that before they went to Bombay, a bhangra boy had mentioned a government-run thermal power plant, where a portion of jobs was reserved for Dalits.

The bhangra kid too had lost his job after the terrorists banned dancing and had advised Bheem to try his luck there.

***

A woman in a khaki saree stood at the door, 'I have come to help you move your things to the women's hostel.'

For three days, nobody came for Shamsie and she left the room only to go to the canteen. What had happened was bizarre. Bheem had left her alone. If she did not know him the way she did, she might have thought it to be a practical joke. Or a manipulative gesture to make her come around. But that would not have been like him at all. In fact, she had no clue how he would act if they differed on something as big as this, because it had never happened before. She also did not know how to deal with a situation where she would be all on her own. Bheem had been a given by her side since she was five. The only constant in her life. She had her mood swings, migraines, her sleep-walking, even her drinking. Bheem had no variations. Even his songs, his need to sing in a full voice, his odd fondness for canals had always been there, even when he was a child.

Shamsie struggled to get accustomed to what had just happened, at least just enough to think clearly. He had not written or called, nor had Sidhu, which meant Bheem had not even told him. There was a phone in the lobby and it would have been easy to find the *dera*'s number if anybody had tried.

Other than the afternoon she had seen him on TV two years ago carrying a dead child, she had never worried for him. He was predictable, present where he was supposed to be, available when he was expected to be.

He was friendly, but had no friends. It is true that during their first stint in Bombay when he had a job and she did not, she had been jealous of the girls in the bar. However, that had been just her feeling excluded.

After the perplexity, came anger, a lashing fury, in which she blamed him for reducing her to one-half of a whole and then tearing himself away without warning and for no sensible rhyme or reason. They were the ones in need. Even if it was Sidhu's idea, he had been keen too. If he had not agreed, they would not have come. What did he expect? To live in a community without following its rules? This was not the city. It was a religious *dera*. Then came a thought that hit her where it hurt most. Why did he react the way he did to the idea of marrying her now or even later? Was it the very idea of marriage? It was true they had never discussed it, even in jest. But was it not understood that they would get married? Is that not what couples did eventually? In fact, he was the one who was so fond of children. Was this a fear of being tamed, of being made to do things, even if it were the thing they would have done anyway. Or was it just a cover for a fierce independence that even he was not aware about? Even then, what was the great harm in at least thinking about marriage? Meanwhile, they could have continued to live in the same campus, even if in different buildings. Even now they had ended up being at different places, she here and he, only God knew where.

She realized it had been three days and she had not been contacted about the job by anyone. She then remembered that they were the ones who had asked for time to think and get back to Ramola. She also remembered that most of their luggage was still in the cloakroom at the railway station. All she had in the bag with her were three sets of clothes. They had repacked in a hurry that morning at the Doctor Sahib's house and some of her undergarments were in Bheem's backpack that he had taken with him. She felt irritated at herself and, for the first time, a sense of awkwardness about the situation. She had no money on her at all, not a single rupee, since it had always been Bheem who carried money when they were together. When she went out alone, she carried a small leather clutch. Her anger at Bheem came back, for leaving her penniless in a strange place. She rummaged at the bottom of the bag hoping desperately that the clutch was there. Instead, she found a wad of five hundred-rupee notes, tied with one of the hair bands she had kept on her bedside the night before Bheem had gone. Seeing the money, she cried for the first time in three days.

And she remembered a hot June afternoon in an air-conditioned cinema hall, when she was 13. As they grew up, whenever school finished early, Shamsie and Bheem would walk to the Bhakra canal through the fields. They spent hours playing, doing homework, and swimming. Bheem would lustily sing his songs just for her. It was a wide canal and the water flowed fast. They stayed near the bank where it was cool under the overhanging trees. When it was too hot for them to walk back across the fields, and if Bheem had money from Batta's house, they would cross the highway and flag a tempo which would stop for them even if it were full. Bheem would share the driver's seat, who did not mind, and Shamsie would sit on the edge of the back seat between women who did mind, but kept quiet. They would then go to the town 10 km away. The gateman at the Ritz would look at their school uniforms unapprovingly, but let them in. The three hours spent in the air-conditioned hall watching a thrilling movie on a wide screen was awe-inspiring for both.

That afternoon, during one such movie show, Shamsie shook Bheem's shoulder and asked him to come out with her, as she was ill. She took him to the ladies' toilet and told him she was having pain in her belly and was bleeding, even though she was not hurt. She proceeded to show him, but Bheem stopped her saying that he knew what it was. He made her sit down in the lobby and told her calmly what he knew.

When a boy grows up in a 12x12 room with his parents, he ends up learning many things without being told. The rest he hears from boys of his age. Shamsie, on the other hand, did not have a mother. She was also shunned by the upper caste girls in her school for being a low caste, and by the Vehra girls for being too uppity and going to a high caste school. Bheem ran out in the blistering sun and into the crowded bazaar, dodging autos and cars. He brought back a pack of cotton and a strip of Saridon. Soon, they were back in the coolness of the hall, and Bheem updated her about the parts she had missed, because he had heard the story from the Vehra boys.

***

A month later, Shamsie joined the job at the *dera* that required training school children how to dance. For weeks, she hated the job for what it had cost her.

The accompanists were Murari, the tabla player, and Sita Ram, the harmonium master. Both had retired from the government publicity department and both lived on campus with their children going to the same school. Both were accomplished, but lacked range. Both were ardent followers of the Mahaprabhu and touched their right ear lobe with thumb and forefinger every time they mentioned him. Both wore a pendant of the Mahaprabhu's picture in a plastic frame around their neck, which had the wearer's photo and an ID number. Shamsie got hers three days after she joined. All the staff and the students were required to wear it. Anybody without it was treated as a visitor, and not as a resident, and would be politely escorted to a buggy and left beyond the inner gate, which visitors were not supposed to cross. Until an ID was organized for them by the security at the gates, the person stayed there.

Twenty-two

Bheem drove his motorcycle at a crawling speed, because he could not see beyond a few feet even at 8 in the morning. The dark grey amalgam of winter fog and smoke from the thermal power plant he worked at blocked his visibility, irritated the eyes, and made breathing an effort. The massive power plant and the many buildings which housed its paraphernalia were spread over a large part of the city. The three giant chimneys, flared wide open at the top, dominated the skyline like the three demons on Dussehra, and belched clouds of black smoke day and night. In winters, the cold air got mixed with the heavy smoke from chimneys, making it settle on anything and everything. A dark layer of soot covered the top of cars, clothes left out to dry, and even the faces of people walking on the street. The railway line, made just for the rumbling trains that brought coal for the power plant from distant collieries of the country, passed through the city.

Bheem had been working as a security guard at the power plant for over three months. He worked in shifts rotating morning, afternoon, and night. He had not called

Shamsie, or anybody else. He missed her as one would miss a body part, but he did not want to come in the way of the dance that she lived for. He was convinced that living in the *dera* was not for him, it would be too stifling. He could not imagine being one of a herd, being shepherded by the likes of Mahaprabhu, even for Shamsie's sake. Or so he told himself. Shamsie had always understood him better than anyone else and he was baffled by how she could not understand how he felt. He had never been good with words, but she knew that too. It was the anger about having to explain himself, when she should have known anyhow, that made him leave while she slept. The exasperation had ebbed now. He was relieved, because he did not know he had it in him to be this angry with her; it had felt awkward while it lasted, as if he was carrying a stranger's baggage. On some days, he almost called Sidhu to let him know where he was, so that Shamsie could join him when she had had enough of the *dera*. But he would not tell him they had fought, otherwise, Sidhu would leave everything and come rushing to put him and Shamsie in a room to sort things out, so that they could be together.

He was getting late for work and for an interview that would promote his job to that of a supervisor. His boss had recommended him for the position even though he was junior to the other two applicants. Stuck at the railway crossing, waiting for the second coal train to pass, he was hemmed in by traffic, with no chance now to turn around and take the detour, which had an underpass below the railway line.

When he finally reached the office, he was met with hostile stares from the other two candidates, who were Jats and had been nice to him until the day before. As he came to know later, the interview had been cancelled because of a fresh government notification that reserved the slot for Scheduled Caste candidates. Bheem, as the only such candidate available, stood automatically selected. The other two hopefuls suspected that Dera Garibparvar had something to do with this change, since Bheem had been seen at the *dera* gate with a girl several weeks ago by a cleaner who worked at the power plant.

The next morning, at 4 am, when it was pitch dark except for the headlight of an oncoming train on the other line, a construction worker from Bihar who was crossing the tracks to relieve himself found a profusely bleeding man lying on the gravel with both his legs cut off above the knees by an earlier train. It seemed he had been heavily sedated and left on the railway line, but had regained just enough consciousness to wriggle himself away, except his legs, one of which had a mole that helped him make out left from right.

After the Dalit workers at the plant went on a strike, the police arrested the two Jat boys. They were subsequently released, because both were able to establish their presence 200 km away, at one of their in-laws' house, on the night of the incident.

The power plant arranged for Bheem's treatment and for prosthetic limbs from the government orthopaedic workshop. The initial visits, measurements, waiting for it to be prepared, the process of the body getting used to the loss first, and then, to the artificial attachments took long. For all those months, Bheem did not go out, not only because he could not, not without the help of others, but also because he did not want to. He felt too conspicuous. He moved around the house with the help of crutches donated to the orthopaedics department by a philanthropist. There was a mismatch with his height and he hardly used those. He never got around to informing Sidhu, and through him Shamsie, about his whereabouts as he had planned to that drab and sooty morning waiting at the railway crossing. When the thought did strike him again, he did not want to.

For the first time, he felt the dark shadow of self-doubt over his mind. If he had not left the *dera* in a huff, he would not have lost his legs. This time, he did not blame Shamsie for having stayed back; he realized it was he who had walked out.

He hardly slept those few months because of the pain in his missing legs, as if the legs were bent at knees in awkward positions. But he could not straighten them, because they were not there. The painkillers did not help. It was a brain thing, they said, the brain takes time to adjust to the fact that the legs are no longer there. That makes two of us, he thought. After a couple of months, the phantom pains started retracting and shrinking into themselves until all that was left were sensations from the stumps of his thighs.

After another month, he asked himself out of mere curiosity, if he could turn back time, would he still choose to leave the *dera* that morning leaving Shamsie behind? He was not surprised to know that the answer was still a 'yes'.

***

Bheem was given the job of sitting in an office and preparing duty rosters of security guards. The crude prostheses cut into his stumps and he threw them away. Since the government implied it had done its duty by him and no more help should be expected, Bheem sold his motorcycle to buy a wheelchair and a pair of proper crutches. The wheelchair was like a small cycle rickshaw with hand pedals. The trade unions found a poster boy in Bheem. The Dalit unions projected him as a mascot of upper caste brutality. A handsome young man, with both legs amputated, singing rousing songs from a wheelchair, fitted the bill perfectly. Bheem obliged, not because he liked the adulation and his picture on posters, but because he got to sing the songs he wanted to and as loudly as he willed before an audience of hundreds who clapped after every verse.

Soon he was called by the general manager, who flashed one of those posters at him and said that while the management encouraged genuine trade union activities, incitement of workers against the government with an armed rebellion already going on amounted to sedition. If it happened again, Bheem would be dismissed from his job at the very least.

When Sidhu tried to look for Bheem later, he came to know that it was around this time that he started to behave oddly. Neighbours would be disturbed at night by the formerly aloof man on his crutches singing at the top of his voice from his terrace. When asked to stop, he warned them of the revolution that was around the corner by singing Faiz at them:

'Ae khaak nasheeno uth baitho woh waqt qareeb
aa pahuncha hai
Jab takht giraye jaaenge, jab taaj uchhale jaaenge'
(You men of the dust, wake up from your
slumber,
The time has come when thrones will tumble,
and crowns kicked around)

He sang such songs at a crowded traffic crossing, standing on his crutches on the podium under the cement umbrella meant for the traffic policeman. And in early mornings, he sat by the Verka milk booth in his wheelchair, when housewives and men on their way back from their walk came to collect milk and, later, at the railway crossing, as people on the way to work waited for the train to cross. On the fourth such day, a police Gypsy came with sirens blazing, cut through the traffic and carried Bheem, and his wheelchair, away.

Twenty-three

The cycle of terrorism was at its bloodiest when Bheem was taken away by the police. An election had been held recently under the shadow of army guns. A small fraction of voters came, brought in by police jeeps to the election booths. However, the law did not specify a minimum polling percentage for an election to be valid.

The new Chief Minister came from a village and knew that the insurgents were running low on both morale and funds at that time. That did not mean they could not get huge amounts of money soon. The Chief Minister sensed that people were tired and would support the state once they saw the tide turning and were no longer afraid. If there ever was an opportune window for the militancy to be crushed, it was then. He appointed a police chief who passionately believed in the old saying, 'Antidote of a poison is another poison.' He made it clear that he would shoot first and ask questions later. He promised results if there was no interference, not even from the Chief Minister. This was readily accepted.

Mayhem broke out, with hundreds of young men picked up every day on suspicion of being terrorists, taken far into the fields at night, and just shot. The police were not after information now. They were after bodies. Guns were placed in lifeless hands, fingers curled around triggers, and shots fired. Each of them had supposedly shot at the police when cornered. Since the policemen were highly trained, they had managed to avoid injuries to their own bodies or so the story went. Some of those killed were real terrorists. Many were not. There was a couple with their toddler returning home on a scooter, after shopping for groceries at the nearby town. They were stopped by the police at a roadblock. The next morning, the child was handed over safe and sound by the police to the perplexed sarpanch of a village located 50 km away from that site. According to a press release, an 'armed encounter' had occurred at midnight near that village, far away from the couple's own village. It seems the couple had been on the run and shot at the police. The newspapers carried this statement and described the dead couple to be high ranking terrorists. Nobody had the time or patience to ask why a terrorist couple would shoot at the police party, while carrying a small child. It eventually turned out to be a case of mistaken identity. The real terrorist couple had slipped across to Nepal, and then flown to Pakistan, on their way to Grenada.

Premium was on the numbers killed. The incentive this time was not cash, but promotions. A jump of two ranks for every five dead bodies, three ranks for 10, four for 20, and so on. It seems that there was a ready-reckoner at the head office to calculate this. There were pickpockets and drug addicts known to the police for years, who suddenly turned out to be deadly terrorists. There was an illegal foreign exchange dealer with a bag full of dollars moving around furtively in a small town on the eastern border of the state. He was found dead, shot in the back at the western end of the state near the Pakistan border. Nobody knew what happened to the bag of hundred-dollar bills.

In that broad sweep, many terrorists too got killed. Others slunk away to Pakistan or Nepal or flew to Grenada and America on forged passports.

It was at the crest of this hurricane that Bheem was brought before the Maai-baap of 'the City of Chimneys', for the crime of singing seditious songs at busy traffic crossings. Maai-baap had not slept the whole night and it showed in his red eyes. It had been a hectic day and a night of shouting orders about the destiny of men who had been lifted away on suspicion of being terrorists in his area. It was a monotonous job and almost always the orders were, '*Gaddi charhao jee*', please put him on a train. Which, of course, meant, take him far away into a field, leave him, and when he runs, shoot him in the back.

After listening to the junior officer's report about Bheem singing Naxalite songs at public places and his being the son of a Dalit communist leader who had been jailed several times, his terse remark in Punjabi was, '*Ik maachod siapa khatam nahin hoea, dooja bhainchod pehlan shuru hon laggya-e.*' What he said in his sleep-deprived irritated manner was that while one mother-fucker ultra-right militancy had not yet come to an end, another sister-fucker ultra-left rebellion was already raising its ugly head.

And then, '*Nipp in the budd, jee. Bhai sahib nu express gaddi charhao.*' Put the brother on a fast train.

The orders were later modified by Maai-baap himself with a slight variation. Adding the body count of a leftist terrorist for promotion under a departmental scheme that was focused on countering the right-wing militancy was bound to be challenged by a rival officer with an equal score, because there were only so many ranks at the top, and everybody could not be promoted. And Bheem had been singing songs at trade-union-arranged gatherings and was known to be a left-wing poster boy. It was thus decided that his body could not be counted for claim to promotion.

The next night, a police Gypsy stopped in the middle of the Satluj bridge and Bheem's legless body, with a single shot at the back of his head, was hoisted away into the river below. When the two men returned to the jeep to drive off, the one in the passenger seat remembered something and asked the driver to wait. He got out and saw the wheelchair at the back of the jeep mocking him. The man looked perplexed at the incriminating wheels of the upside down wheelchair, until both the simplicity and appropriateness of the solution struck him. He dragged the wheelchair out and threw it as far into the swirling waters as he could.

Bheem was not a terror suspect. It was neither a case of mistaken identity, nor was he killed for the purpose of a promotion.

He just happened to be in the path of a raging tornado.

***

The night Bheem was killed, Shamsie was in London as a part of the cultural troupe of Dera Garibparvar, staying at a hotel near the airport. They had come there a week back and had already been to Birmingham and Leister, cities with high concentrations of Punjabis. In the evening, they had performed at an auditorium where the Indian community of London had facilitated Mahaprabhu. The troupe was to fly home the next morning. On the bus back to the hotel, Ramola informed Shamsie in a tone which was both congratulatory and envious that the Mahaprabhu was impressed with her work and would come to her room to congratulate her in person, after he was free from meeting some local Souls who had been waiting in the hotel lobby.

'Keep the door unlocked. He does not like to wait,' she advised.

It did not come as a surprise to Shamsie. There had been vibes throughout the trip. His hand lingering on her head while blessing and then an incidental brush against the cheek. Lifting her by her arms when she bowed to touch his feet on stage, and leaving them there for two seconds longer than necessary.

Shamsie did not go to her room. Instead, she spent the night with two of her students. At 5 in the morning, she was in the lobby with her bags along with everyone else as required. On the flight back, she did not talk to anybody.

Two days later, Shamsie left the *dera* for good. At the gate, she handed over a token and demanded back the bottle of whisky and the pack of cigarettes that had been taken out of her baggage. They were returned to her sealed and numbered in a plastic cover. She remembered Bheem saying the day before he left that the devil was more organized than god.

By the afternoon, she had found Sidhu. They met at a teashop outside Dhakka Colony. It was a small state; how long could it possibly take to find Bheem they thought. Shamsie bought a camp cot and started living in the office. At night, she would be alone in the giant shell of a building. It is not that she did not feel safe there. What was safe in those days anyway; even cosy houses with three-tiered security could be death traps. It was the stark loneliness, lying on a camp cot in that humongous brick and mortar honeycomb that gnawed at her mind.

At first, I could not recognize her. Her silhouette stood there framed in the door of my clinic and I could not see her face clearly. From the slouching posture, I took her to be a middle-aged woman with the nasty viral fever, which was going around and which sapped one's energy in just a day. It was mid-morning and I had already seen a dozen patients. It was just then that Sidhu entered. I knew it was something far more serious than a viral fever. They had come to ask if I knew anything about Bheem's whereabouts, if he had by any chance come to see me. They had already gone to all his friends he could have met or called, and they were not many.

'I thought he would have called me at least,' Sidhu looked worried and hurt.

Shamsie's hair was dishevelled. She had tried to tie it with a rubber band, but had failed to gather it all. She looked as if she had not slept for days and had been crying. It was a version of Shamsie I had never seen or imagined.

When there was no sign of Bheem even after a week, Shamsie hired a room in Dhakka Colony. It was easy to get rooms since hundreds of Bihari labourers, who lived there on rent, four to one in a room, had recently fled the state after being attacked at the brick kilns where they worked. It took Shamsie and Sidhu more than a month to find any lead on Bheem. Then an acquaintance who knew Bheem remembered seeing a poster with the picture of somebody looking like him in a wheelchair. Shamsie's heart sank. She did not believe it to be true but, at the same time, did not want to be the one to find out. It was left to Sidhu to go to the city with the giant chimneys in search of Bheem.

The neighbours reported that Bheem had gone for work one morning in his wheelchair and never returned. An old woman, who lived two houses away and sold car fresheners at the railway crossing, said she had seen a police jeep take away a man in a wheelchair. At the police station, Sidhu hit a stonewall. Nobody had ever seen or heard of a man in a wheelchair. 'Not at least during my 10 years of working here,' the guard at the entrance said.

'I would have remembered, no? How many men without legs get arrested that I would forget?' the munshi at the police station said. He quickly went through the register, looking for a name as if to humour Sidhu. 'I told you,' he concluded after two minutes.

The old cobbler on the street outside the police station waved him down and advised, 'Every day, mothers, wives, and fathers come here looking for their relatives. But nobody has seen them. And nobody will, trust me. I have been sitting at this spot for 20 years. I know what goes on in there. Try to forget him if you can is all I have to say. Because what else can you do?'

Twenty-four

One year had passed since I was admitted under Dr Mustafa for the psychotic episode triggered by my detention in cell number 6 at the waterlogged Satluj Range Police Station. My diagnosis was revised from Unipolar Depression to Bipolar Disorder, which meant I was prone to not just bouts of depression, but also grandiose excitements. Unless put on maintenance mood stabilizers, I would be swinging from one extreme to the other like a yo-yo for the rest of my life. I was started on a drug called Lithium. After years of recurrent troughs, my mood flattened and stayed like that whatever the season. Jeet said it became like water in the cement lined Sirhind canal, which stays at a fixed watermark, unlike earlier when it was like water in the river that ebbed and flowed every few days.

It was a relief from the perpetual dread of wondering what mood I would be in the next morning when I woke up. Dr Mustafa said he wished that the police torture had happened earlier. I said I wished it had happened to him. We talked on a more equal level now, a relationship that develops between a psychiatrist and the patient who has been stable for long.

The flatness of stability did not come for free. Stability never does. Mine came at the cost of the sheer intensity of feelings. I no longer felt stuck or down in the dumps, but I missed feeling the pain and worry of my patients as before. I was certainly more clinical and efficient and saw more patients. My patients clearly preferred this version of me, more predictable and less irritable. I was balanced, but there was something important missing.

'I have not cried for a whole year for God's sake,' I complained to Dr Mustafa, 'and I miss it. I cannot cry even if I try.'

'Seriously, so now we are crying over not being able to cry. I mean who does that?' he joked.

'Trust you to find something to moon over, even this.' Another time, he said that flatness of emotions had been reported with mood stabilizers, but he had never seen anyone complain about it. 'That is you, the ultimate introspective introvert.'

It was about 6 pm and already dark that December evening. Fog had set in early. An unexpected visitor dropped in to meet me and I was surprised to see Sidhu, whom I had met just once, years ago. This time, he was not wearing his kirpan. Since the visibility had gone down abruptly because of the fog, I suggested that he stayed the night. He parked his car inside the gate. After we had dinner and after I wondered why he had not said anything about Bheem and Shamsie despite their being his only connection to me, I asked if he knew where they were.

Instead, he told me he was no longer religious because faith had failed him. He poured whisky from a bottle he brought from his car and started to tell me about what had been happening to them since the day they entered the *dera*. Sidhu was a good raconteur. He went into details. Parts of his account he had heard from others and this, he admitted conscientiously, as he went forward in his attempt to update me.

By the time he reached the point where Bheem started singing songs of revolution from his terrace at night, it was 1 in the morning, and Sidhu had finished half his bottle.

Shamsie had gone into a shell after she came to know about Bheem having been in a wheelchair and then lifted away by police for singing Faiz. A month later, she told Sidhu that she wanted to search more. She argued that all the men shot by the police, whether real or fake terrorists, had their bodies found since promotions required a body count. So where was Bheem's body if he was shot by them? They spent three months visiting police stations in and around 'the City of Chimneys'. They went to the High Court in exile and filed a petition for habeas corpus. The government replied in all truthfulness that they had gone through all the records and no such person had ever been arrested by the police and that they had not been able to find him, dead or alive, despite the court's order. A lawyer who had filed many such petitions told them that there were thousands who had not been found, either dead or alive. When the number of promotions based on body counts had reached a scandalous level, the scheme had been abolished. However, the police still had the remnants of an insurgency to wipe out. The bodies were then cremated by the police as unclaimed.

Shamsie and Sidhu spent many days going around the cremation grounds, rummaging through their registers for any record of Bheem. Then they met a man who swore he had seen the police throw a dead body without legs into the river, followed by a wheelchair. He remembered the date well, because he had gone to the bridge that night to consign to the river the ashes of his dead wife.

That was the day when Sidhu put his kirpan away and started drinking. And Shamsie stopped. She knew in her heart that if she had not been stubborn about the *dera*, Bheem would still be alive. There was no escape from that truth and there never would be. For two months, Sidhu stayed home drinking and Shamsie stayed in her room without meeting anybody.

Life in the state had steadily come to an even keel, although, according to a survey by a fact-finding organization, more than 8,000 persons, mostly young men, had still not come back home, dead or alive, after their disappearance one year ago.

Night buses had started plying and late shows in cinemas became full. Jobs came back to Dhakka Colony. Every evening, waiters dressed like penguins trooped into the city. Canters and music bands with dancing girls shot out of the narrow lanes, making their way to the inner city, towns, and villages.

Three months later, Sidhu convinced Shamsie to cobble together Jassi orchestra from scratch. She agreed, but said she would just be a dance teacher and would not be dancing on stage.

People, long starved of splurging, had a lot of catching up to do. There was a backlog of weddings, engagements, anniversaries, and parties that had all been waiting for things to come back to normal.

The orchestra was booked for weeks in advance even without Shamsie dancing. Some clients still asked for her, but Sidhu managed those queries deftly.

***

It was a cold night. My bed was on the side of the road, and through the narrow crevices in the wood of the window frame, the chilling breeze was managing to come in. I had to wrap the quilt even more tightly around me. Earlier, I had brought wood from the terrace and started a fire in the fireplace, which I rarely used. Sidhu was sitting cross-legged on his bed with a blanket wrapped around him. He had been drinking slowly for the last one hour and there was still some whisky left.

He poured all of that in his glass in one go to make a large purple drink.

Last week, a client called for a booking for a wedding, but insisted they were interested only if Shamsie herself would come.

'We want her, because she is from our village. She grew up here. It is the musical night for my son's wedding. Your party is invited to stay for the wedding at the village gurudwara, till the next morning. We will arrange for your stay. My son insists, please see if you can do anything.'

That one drink had done to Sidhu's speech what the whole night of drinking had not. I had to make an effort to understand what he was saying.

I managed to piece together that after knowing the wedding was in her village, she had agreed. In fact, she was quite excited about it. Bheem was not coming back, she told herself, and it was their village, where the two of them had been born, played marbles, then Chhatapu, then gully cricket. They had gone to school there. Whenever Bheem nicked money from the Batta teacher's house, they had eaten jalebis. Yes, she would go there and dance. One last time.

The music night to celebrate the wedding was not in the village proper, but in a newly-opened resort on the highway next to where their school had been. The school itself had been replaced by a row of tractor spare part shops. The road was almost blocked by the haphazardly parked cars of wedding guests. The resort had an auditorium with a stage and built-in speakers, and Sidhu had to just plug in his equipment. Shamsie had been jittery; it was her village and there would be people she grew up with, her class fellows from the school, and everybody would be somebody she knew. She had swallowed the propranolol pill for stage fright that she had carried along. She was going to dance after a year, but that was the last thing she was anxious about. That part would come she was sure. When she went on stage, all she felt was a dull emptiness. She danced well, but it was mechanical. All the moves were right, but she did not feel a thing. The hall was full of inebriated men, and women dressed in shiny dresses and clunky jewellery. There were catcalls and some requests for more, to which she obediently complied. Nobody seemed to know that she was from that village. At least, nobody mentioned it. The groom did not seem to be there, although his parents and sisters sat in the front row. Sidhu heard he was having a bachelors' party with his buddies at another place in the same resort.

They stayed in the guest rooms in the same complex, but on different floors. Shamsie had agreed to stay, because she wanted to go to the stupas in the morning and walk through the Vehra in the daylight and attend the wedding. She wanted to go as an invited guest to the same big gurudwara, from where she and Bheem had been thrown out as children. And of course, she had to go to the museum and return to them something that was rightfully theirs.

From the window of her room, she could see the pale lights atop the gate of the museum, where her father had worked for eight years, cleaning the toilets outside the main halls, but was not allowed to sweep the floors of the museum where the priceless artefacts were displayed in glass cases under reflected lights. Because he was not born clean enough to dust the glass cases of the majestic Shalabhanjikas.

He cleaned the toilets outside the hall till he was killed by the beedis he smoked, which he had once quit to become a true Sikh and started again after being told he would still be a Chamar.

She could make out the road in the moonlight, even the T-junction that went straight to the bazar, which was common to four villages and from where they bought jalebis every time Bheem had money.

She saw through the window myriad sets of colourful lights perched on a hillock, which would be the groom's house in the village Uccha Pind, which was her village too, at least the Vehra part was.

She was awake even an hour after she had been in bed, when there was a rustle and a scrape at the door. She sprang up to sit straight, her heart thudding. When the door half opened, the hallway light showed a man enter quickly. Then the door clicked shut. She clearly remembered having locked it.

Shamsie screamed, but no voice came out of her. Then a heavy, abrasive palm pressed down hard on her mouth, pushing her head back against the pillow. She struggled to breathe and, in that moment, when she felt she was dying of suffocation, she saw the silhouette of the man in her room from the flitting light of a passing car on the road. She knew the man who was weighing down on her body, with his other hand gripping tight her wrists at her back. It was Sukha, who had pinned her down, just like now, in the fields, not far from that room, more than 10 years ago. He eased the pressure on her mouth and hissed breathlessly, 'You will be paid as much as you want. That is what you do anyway.'

She knew then this was not just a drunk man seized by lust. It was a man who had nursed humiliation. It was somebody who had planned. He knew this was certainly not what she did for a living, because then there would have been a transaction. He was not here for that. He was here for revenge. Shamsie now knew that Sidhu's room being on another floor was part of the plan. In that moment, she also knew that with the windows sealed shut, the room heater with the noisy blower on, and the hallway deserted, she had to fight alone.

He forced her face towards him and Shamsie braced herself while struggling to turn her face away. Instead of kissing her, he slapped her hard on the cheek.

'This is what you deserve, not a kiss. What do you Chamar girls think of yourselves anyway? That you will hit a Jat boy, break his tooth, and he will just forget about it? What I wanted that day in the fields has been happening for centuries. What was so strange in that? You would have liked it too. It wasn't just about me.'

Her mind stunned after the slap, she could not struggle for a while. He had to just stretch his arm to pull her chunni trailing from the back of the chair in the room. With that, he tied her wrists at the back and forced her to sit in the chair, pressing her mouth with a hand just in case. He loosened his belt with one hand to let his trousers and then his underwear drop to his feet, pushing her back against the chair with the other hand. Then he tried to force himself into her mouth. When she clenched her teeth to resist, he slapped her, and then backslapped her again,

'You thought, I was going to fuck you. No, you do not deserve that either. Pay me back for my tooth this way and then we would be even, I promise.'

During the few seconds she went limp, he managed to push his now erect penis into her mouth.

He was holding her head and moving it back and forth. Shamsie was alert again and felt a nauseous bile rising from her stomach. Then in a moment of aversion, shame, anger, hate, and clarity, she tightened her mouth and dug her teeth deliberately and determinedly into the stiff flesh. Sukha erupted into obscenities. He tried to withdraw, which hurt even more. Sukha's hands went around her neck in a desperate attempt to strangle her, but the all-consuming pain had numbed his brain and weakened his grasp.

The pain had made the penis softer and that made the teeth go through it easier. Blood was spouting from Shamsie's mouth and going back into her throat, some of which she had to swallow.

Her teeth pressed one final time to avenge for her humiliation of that day, for not being allowed into the gurudwara as a child, for her father having been cheated and driven to death, for his great-grandfather having been forced to jump off a cliff and, most of all, for Bheem's legs, and then, for his life.

Sukha had collapsed and doubled over her shoulder. Her teeth met. She spat out the glob of flesh and blood and pushed him away. When he slumped to the floor moaning with pain, pressing himself with both his hands to stem the flow of blood, she stood up and spat again with all the force she had. With her fingers, she managed to loosen the knot on her chunni and darted into the bathroom. The front of her dress was soaked in blood. She was horrified to see her lips, teeth, and tongue the colour of dark red with blood running down her chin and neck. She washed in a desperate hurry, but knew there was no time to change. Sukha was conscious, but still unable to get up from the floor. She found her slippers, opened the door, and ran towards the stairs. She was wrong about there being nobody in the hall at that time of the night. There was a man in a guard's uniform, a look out brought by Sukha. He knew right away that the blood on the girl's dress had to be his master's and rather than following her, he had to go and help him.

A pouring rain had started meanwhile, washing down some of the blood on her shirt. Shivering because of the cold and fear, Shamsie ran to the back of the hotel, behind the shops, and to the village road. The rain was a torrent now and she remembered walking on the same road in a similar flash rain when classes had been suspended, because the school roof had started leaking, and the back of her salwar had become mud-splattered because of her rubber flip flops. However, the road was metalled now. She kept running in the dark and turned towards the village. There were car lights appearing in the distance, and soon, there were sounds of vehicles muffled by the rain and thunder. The lights and sounds came nearer. There were shouts and gunshots. Her hope of getting to the Vehra and asking for help gone, she ran in the direction of the ruin of the Buddhist monastery.

She heard more gunshots and felt something cling to her midriff and when she touched it to see, it was warm blood. She crawled under the barbed wire, like she would do with Bheem on their way back from school and was pinned down under the headlights at that moment. There were shouts and curses. She managed to crawl over the 2-feet-high remnants of a wall and fell bleeding on the floor of the two-thousand-year-old prayer hall. Shamsie started crawling towards the other side of the stupa, where there was a gap in the fence. The headlights lost her for a few seconds and she was now running in a freshly ploughed field. But soon, the lights found her again and, from across the prayer hall, she was shot at, several times, as vengeful men would do. There was a long spell of thunder and lightning and sheets of water poured down, as if the sky had split open.

And then, she was a child of nine and there was the majestic figure of bronze, larger by a million times and not static, but dancing a divine dance across the heavens from one edge of the horizon to the other, on a screen as vast as the sky. The thunder was now celestial music and stunning patterns of lightening adorned the entire sky. She heard the voice call to her, a call she had been hearing since she was a child. Only this time, it was louder and clearer, 'Come after me. Let us go and dance. In a hall even bigger.'

Sidhu found Shamsie within a few minutes of being shot, lying in a field. There was another flash of lightening and he saw something had fallen out of her hand. It was a delicate brass figurine of a girl in a graceful dancing pose. The same figurine Shamsie had found as a child in the same freshly ploughed field probably at the same spot where she had fallen.

Before sleep took over, Sidhu said that Shamsie had been in coma for a week and doctors had given up on her. Sukha had lost a lot of blood, but was likely to improve enough to go home soon.

Sidhu was asleep, slumped in the bed, neither sitting nor lying. It was probably dawn, but there was no light to show for it. A surge of fog was striking against the panes like a crazed animal.

There was a laborious creak of a bicycle chain from the road. An old man driving an old bicycle.

The raspy singsong voice coupled with the creaking of the chain, carried clearly across the fog.

'Ik onkar satt naam kartapurakh,
Nir bhau, nirvair, akal murat, ajuni, saibhang,
gurprasad.
Aad sach jugaad sach
Hai bhi sach,
Nanak hosee bhi sach.'

(There is one God, eternal truth is His name, He is the creator, fearless, without enmity, shapeless, beyond birth and death, true in the primal beginning, true through eons, here and everywhere.)

Shamsie had been giving me gifts of liquor bottles over the years, which I never drank. That cold and lightless morning, she gave me the gift of my lost ability to cry, which I hold close to my heart even today, more than any medicines Dr Mustafa ever prescribed.

Epilogue

The comatose Shamsie, who the doctors had given up on, eventually survived. Sukha, who was to be discharged soon, developed a fulminating infection of the stitched wound and died. The most dangerous of all bites is the human bite, nurses reminded one another.

Shamsie is now an adored Dalit icon, although she does not take that position very seriously. She spends most of her time at the dancing school she runs. She has trained teachers, pays them well, and lives in the same building as them.

Sidhu is married to a Jat girl from a rich landed family known to his father and has a son. He lives in Sector 3 of Chandigarh and has joined the political party of opium eaters. He has been baptized once again and has quit drinking.

More than eight thousand young men have not come home. And never will.

Shamsie meets me whenever she passes my way in her Maruti Zen. If it is late, she stays over.

On this autumn evening, when the sky is full of stars and the river has submerged half of the *sarkanda* grass, she asks me, 'What caste are you from?'

She is going to speak at a convention of farm labourers the next morning.

I have always been uncomfortable around this question and give my stock reply.

'I hate identities.'

'And that, Doctor Sahib, is the difference. You have the privilege to hate identities and say it too, and that privilege comes with your caste. If I said I hate identities, I would be told, of course you do, you are a Chamar. Therefore, I cannot even say that. Not in this birth. I hope that I am born a Jat or a Brahmin next time just for the sake of this one privilege. The privilege of being able to say I hate identities. Right now, I have to hug my identity close to my chest and tell others like me to do the same.'

'Is this what you are going to speak about tomorrow?' I ask.

'That too, but I do not speak much. I sing songs like Bheem did. Not as well, but I am trying.'

Looking beyond the river as if searching for someone, she sang a few lines in a voice that was deep and stirring,

'Words have been uttered

Long before us,

And will be uttered

For long after we are gone

Chop off every tongue

If you can.

But the words have been uttered.'

Acknowledgements

Finding a new publisher all over again during the lean times of a pandemic is not easy and I am thankful to my literary agent, Preeti Gill, for making it possible. I am also thankful to Bani Gill and to Arunima Ghosh of Niyogi Books for the diligent editorial help.

I am grateful to Nirupama Dutt for allowing me to use in the book three stanzas from poems by Lal Singh Dil, as translated by her from Punjabi to English ('Poet of the Revolution: The Memoirs of Lal Singh Dil, Viking').

About the author

Anirudh Kala lives in Ludhiana and is a psychiatrist by profession. His experience as a psychiatrist shows in how he sketches out his characters and their personality traits. This is his second book as a fiction writer, the first being The *Unsafe Asylum: Stories of Partition and Madness* (2018).

His focus is always to educate people about mental health and mental illness, focusing on eradicating stigma, labels, and prejudice.

Besides his professional passions, Anirudh Kala also likes reading Urdu poetry, hiking, and listening to Indian semi-classical music.